LITTLE TRAMP

Also by Tobi Little Deer

LAKE ISLE
Tobi's Vermont countryside adventure

LITTLE TRAMP

An Adventure Story

by

Tobi Little Deer

TOBI Books
New York

TOBI Books
An imprint of Woodwrit, Inc. Editions

ISBN: 978-0-692365-16-8

IN MEMORY OF

TRUMAN

THE NOBLEST GERMAN SHEPHERD

AND

MUFFY

DEVOTED LHASA APSO

AND

FONDLY DEDICATED TO

LUCY AND LOLA

CHIHUAHUAS WITH ATTITUDE

With grateful acknowledgement to
Marilyn, Anthony, and David
for their invaluable help.

CONTENTS

1. THE ATTACK 1

2. THE ACCIDENT 6

3. THE SUPER 10

4. MACK 15

5. WORKING THE STREET 20

6. MADNESS 25

7. AGNES 30

8. ON LEASH AGAIN WITH MANY HOMES 35

9. HEARTBREAK 40

10. HAPPILY WITH AGNES 45

11. JENNY 49

12. THE WHITE DOG — AND COMPANY 55

13. MATHILDE 60

14. MOLLY 67

15. FAMILY 72

16. THE NORTH WOODS 77

17. ACCIDENTS HAPPEN   83

18. THE POOL   88

19. POOR BOY   93

20. DOCTOR FARLAND   97

21. MOTHER   102

22. SUNSHINE   105

23. KIDNAPPED   109

24. ANGELA   114

25. FAMILY DIFFERENCES   119

26. DOG BAIT   123

27. THUNDER   128

28. FIGHT EVENT   133

29. ANIMAL CONTROL   138

30. REUNION   142

31. ABINGTON SQUARE   145

32. BACK TO THE POOL   148

33. THOR   152

34. AND NOW   155

LITTLE TRAMP

1. THE ATTACK

I awoke, pushed my face out of the remains of my homeless shelter, and discovered that it was daylight, really too late to go about alone. Without someone to walk with, I'd have to contend with people trying to grab me.

"Look at that little dog. He's loose!"

Seeing my coloring, they'd ask, "A German Shepherd puppy?"

"No, not with those ears, a Chihuahua. Catch him!"

Lately it was more like, "Check out that scruffy little stray," and they weren't trying so hard anymore. It'd been a while, and I looked like I belonged on the city streets. Still, it was safer to go out after dark.

I was reluctant, too, to leave the warmth I'd created by burrowing into the pile of clothing and soft blankets Agnes had accumulated in the corner of our alleyway, most of them tossed about now. I'd fled after Mack's raid, and I wouldn't have returned at all if I hadn't gotten so cold wandering outside. I had nowhere else to go against the chill, and I remembered how warm it was under the blankets with Agnes. I'll always remember. She'd talk to me or to herself until we both fell asleep. Sometimes I dozed off while she was still speaking. She talked gently. So soothing, it was like soft music.

A day had passed since I lost Agnes, and I missed her very much. Awake, I looked out anxiously and very watchfully, hoping she'd come walking back into the alley, and that Mack wouldn't. I was still trembling from his violence, still very upset that I'd been uprooted once again. It happened so fast, and like every misfortune so unexpectedly.

Agnes and I had just returned from visiting Mathilde uptown, making it back to our alleyway wearily late in the night. We were used to wandering Manhattan, the two of us, and Agnes was tough, but she was an old lady and very tired after the long walk along the river. She'd collapsed on our bed of blankets and coats and pulled them over her. I crawled in beside her as I always did. We were a good sleeping pair, Agnes and I.

Past the deepest hours, in the lingering darkness not long before dawn, I heard someone at the opening to our alley. I looked out, and the shadow I saw silhouetted in dim street light sent a shiver down my back and made me growl angrily. It was mean Mack. He was coming toward us, staggering like a zombie, feeling his way along the wall, so out of his mind he could hardly walk. I snarled, I barked, I sprang from the blankets and ran around him to get away. Mack hesitated for only a moment, as if wondering where the sound was coming from. Standing my ground by the side wall at the alley entrance, braced to escape, I faced back in at him. With fur bristling, I barked furiously to warn Agnes. Mack reached the bulging garbage bags she'd set around our bed. They held all her possessions we'd collected, and he began ripping them open.

By now Agnes was awake. She was on her feet,

crying out to him, "Leave my things alone! Don't you touch them!" She grabbed his arm. He shoved her away, and she fell with a thud, but she had courage. She reached back and grabbed his leg. "Don't touch my things! Don't touch my things!"

"Get off me!" Mack snarled.

Agnes wrapped her arms around Mack's leg so he couldn't shake her off, and kept yelling, "Help! Help! Help!" Her cries and Mack's roars were a horrible noise, her screaming, and his bellowing, and my barking all mixed together. Mack reached down, grabbed Agnes by the throat with one hand, pulled her off him and threw her against the wall. I remembered when he'd done that to me. Agnes slumped down into a pile, silent now, not a whimper. I was so afraid she wouldn't ever wake up. Mack tore through her bags as fast as he could.

I knew I'd better run, and I did, and I only looked back when I was safely a street away. Mack came stumbling out of the alley, pushing past the several people attracted by the ruckus. No one tried to stop him. He probably didn't see me, but he was coming in my direction, so I ran. It wasn't long before I heard an ambulance in the distance. I kept going. There weren't many people on the street at that hour, but those there were looked surprised as I dashed past them, as they always did seeing me free. I darted in and out, following the curb side—"like a fox follows the edge of a field," Ted would say. I ran fast. Being a "deer-head" Chihuahua, I have good running legs, long hind legs that propel me, and I was quick to dodge anyone who reached for me. If I slowed to a trot, some people still tried; but when I galloped, and they'd have to make more effort, they didn't bother. As soon as I got a chance, I found a hiding place.

It was cold winter. There'd been some snow. Streets were mostly clear, but the sidewalks were wet with ice-melt, and the air was frigid damp. I hid under a tarp next to a construction site, which protected me from the wind, but not the chill, and soon I was shivering so much that I could hardly breathe. When I dared to venture out, I stopped on a grating where steam was rising. It heated me, but got me all wet. I couldn't stay there, either, because it was out in the open. I trotted on, ran some, to avoid people and to warm myself. I thought of Agnes and our bed of blankets, and with no other refuge I returned to our alley.

I found our things scattered all over the place. Some had fallen in a pile, including a blanket that Mack had tossed against the wall. I crawled into it. It didn't take long for me to start feeling warmer, buried in heavy cloth, and I soon fell asleep. When I awoke—which is where I began my story—it was daytime. Warmth and caution won over hunger right then, and I dozed again to wait for nightfall.

By twilight I was too hungry to delay any longer, so I came out from under the blanket, the remnant of my home with Agnes, and headed out. There still were people on the street, but I could keep out of sight in the shadows. I trotted down the sidewalk, on the curb side where I couldn't be trapped, in and out around the tree plantings, "like a fox." People were tired at the end of the day, so if I moved fast enough, they didn't reach for me. As always, some were surprised and stopped when I ran by. They looked around to see who had me out off-leash, and by the time they realized there was no one with me, I was gone.

I found half a hamburger that'd fallen over the edge of a trash can, and despite the mustard it tasted so good! I kept moving, from one corner trash can to the next. Sometimes there were appetizing smells, whole meals half-eaten in Styrofoam containers, but I couldn't reach them. I could only get what'd fallen by the side. I found a piece of pizza, almost a whole one. I love pizza. Keeping an eye on people approaching, I began to eat it right there. When someone came too close, I ran with it down the street to a shadowed nook where I scarfed it down undisturbed. After that I felt better.

I trotted on down Seventh Avenue. I didn't have to run anymore as it got darker, so long as I remained outside the glare of the streetlights. When I came to Sheridan Square, I looked across at the bank where I used to go with Ted, and I stopped, because I knew the way home from there so well. We'd walked it together many times. It seemed natural to follow it, towards the building where we lived.

2. THE ACCIDENT

My home in New York City with Ted was the only one I'd known. Now, walking down Grove then Christopher Streets towards it, I quivered with hope as much as from the cold. It was my most precious memory. Our Greenwich Village apartment was a warm place in winter, cool in summer. I had my own little house there set into the bottom of a bedroom bookcase—really a cat house, but it worked fine for a Chihuahua, too. My bed in it was a pillow covered with a lush sheep fleece, and I spent much of my day there in total luxury.

When I reached Waverly Place, I hesitated for a moment in front of Three Lives Bookstore, looking across at the spot near Julius' Bar where I lost my comfortable world so suddenly.

Ted and I had just returned earlier that evening from our house at the beach. We had dinner, and then it was time for our walk. I heard Ted say to me, "Tobi, let's go out." Nothing forewarned me that this short trip around the block would be different from any other. So I rolled onto my back for him to rub my belly. First, a belly rub. Then I came out of my house, stretched, and Ted put my harness on me. He picked me up, and I rode on his arm. Out the door we went; he locked it behind us. That's how we always did it.

Ted carried me to Waverly Place, where he set me

down. "Why are you always carrying that dog?" someone passing by once asked. "I don't want him doing his business on the sidewalk," Ted told her, "and around the corner on Waverly where there's less traffic, I can take him into the street."

I watched other people lead their dogs to front steps, to lamp posts and flower beds, but Ted insisted, "Dogs are supposed to do it in the street." So there we were, four times a day, Ted guiding me along the curb. He had to watch out for every car that came by, because many of them didn't move over very much. That evening one came down Waverly fast and instead of giving us room, drove right at us. Ted swung my leash, so my harness carried me up onto the sidewalk; and he jumped, too— not soon enough—and he flew off its fender. The car swerved, bounced off a vehicle parked on the other side, and kept going. Ted was on the ground; I saw him move a little. I nudged him with my nose so he'd know I was there.

People walking on the opposite side came running. "Call 911," one person shouted, as her partner dialed his phone.

Other people rushed up the sidewalk, and I sprang out of their way. I didn't know these people. Someone cried, "Grab his dog's leash." A man lunged, and I jumped away. Every time he grabbed for my leash trailing behind me, I jumped a few more steps beyond him, so he kept missing it.

A person asked, "How's the guy? What happened?"

Another answered, "He's conscious. He cracked his

head . . ."

I heard Ted say feebly, "My dog . . ."

The man was still trying to catch me, his arms wide apart to corral me in them. I ran across the little park at McCarthy Square.

Someone said, "Forget the dog . . . it's gone."

When the man kept coming after me, I ran up Seventh Avenue.

It was all a blur, pure panic in a totally unknown situation. I'd have stayed with Ted, because I'd never been outside without him. If he dropped my leash, I always stopped for him to pick it up again. That's how we walked down the street, Ted and I, on leash. Now he was lying on the ground surrounded by strangers and paying no attention to me at all. I was alone outside! The confidence I got from Ted, the protection I felt through the leash, vanished when he didn't get up. And all those people rushing at me had me too rattled to stay by.

Ted and I jogged every morning along the river for exercise, so I'm a practiced runner. I ran now up the avenue, not at a lope like mornings, but at full gallop. I was running to get away because I found myself alone without Ted to protect me, but there were people everywhere, all strangers. They looked so surprised when I dashed by. They pointed, "Look at that little dog dragging his leash. Where's his owner?" Some of them grabbed for me, but I dodged and kept running. I was in full flight. No time to think, just to run. I'd never been out on my own before. My heart pounded as I ran away. Soon it got dark, and only then I slowed my pace.

What now? Everything was unfamiliar, and all the same. I could've run and run and never stopped, and there'd always be more avenue. The city kept stretching on ahead. I slowed to a trot. If I kept going, I'd be nowhere. Home was the only place I wanted to be. I turned around and went back the way I'd come, back down Seventh Avenue. Sometimes I walked; sometimes I trotted or ran, even though I felt very tired. I wanted to get home and into my little house, to escape back inside, be safe and fall asleep. That's what I wanted, just to get home.

3. THE SUPER

It was a long walk, but I felt better the closer I got. I began to recognize buildings. Finally in Greenwich Village I knew my way perfectly. I turned down Waverly and passed where it all had happened, but now the street looked like it always did—no sign of Ted or the people who rushed at us. I circled wide around the spot, continued on down the street, and turned the corner. This was the homestretch. I ran to our building, leaped up the four front steps to the landing, and was stopped by the big, closed front door.

The building super, Milan, came by. From the sidewalk he looked at me, puzzled. "What're you doing out here, Tobi? Where's Ted?" he asked me as if I could answer him, or he was thinking out loud. "It's not like Ted to leave you by the door alone even for a minute. Where is he?" I knew Milan was a good man. I was used to him, all the times Ted greeted him and they chatted when they met. He looked up and down the street to see if Ted would appear. After a few moments he repeated, "What's going on? He wouldn't leave you outside alone," then started up the steps towards me. He said, "Let's check it out," and moved to gather me up. He was a good man, but who'd never held me. I jumped away and looked back at him from the sidewalk. I wanted his help, but I was unsure about letting him pick me up. Milan said, "I'm not going to try to chase you if you're going to run." Instead he turned down the outer stairs to his apartment, wondering again aloud to himself, "Where's Ted?"

I returned to the landing in front of the door and waited. I had to get inside to get home. Now and then people opened the door passing through, but too quickly for me. My chance came when the girls in Apartment 1 came out with their boyfriends to smoke. I jumped off the steps out of their way, but I didn't run because they left me alone. When they finished, I followed them through the outer door into the entry, and through the inner door into the hall. They let me be, and they disappeared into their apartment. I was left alone in the hallway. I walked to the stairs. I don't like stairs, ever since I slipped and cracked my chin on them when I was a puppy. Ted always had carried me up since then. So I waited.

Finally I realized that the only way to get home was to climb them. I got up my courage and ran them all at once, not hesitating even at the landings. I tripped a few times, jumped and pulled myself all the way to our apartment on the third floor, where I was stopped again, by the closed door. By now it was very late, way past Ted's and my bedtime. Nobody came or went. The building was quiet, and I fell asleep in front of the door.

Early morning people began to descend the stairs and walk by me. Some of them wondered out loud, "What are you doing there?" However, because I was in front of our apartment, they didn't bother me. I waited patiently for Ted to open the door and find me, and then everything would be back to normal. A long time passed. I got hungry, but it didn't matter; I waited. Eventually Ted would appear.

Much later, I heard Milan coming up the stairway. He hesitated when he saw me, and he said, "Well, Tobi, here you are. Where's Ted?" He came to the door; I didn't feel I had to move. Milan knocked on it twice, then a third time pounded hard. There was no answer. He took out his phone. I could hear ringing in our apartment. Milan stood there waiting, and it rang and rang, and rang, until he put the phone away. He said to me, "You wait, Tobi. I'm going to find out what's going on." He disappeared down the stairs, and I lay down again, but not for long. Milan soon was back with keys; he turned them in the locks, opened the door, and went into our apartment. I ran past him, ran to every room looking for Ted, took a drink of water from my bowl in the kitchen, and then followed Milan again from room to room as he called out to Ted.

Milan looked at me. "Well, little fellow, I don't know what's happened, but Ted's not here. Something not good, I think, or you wouldn't be out loose like that. I'm going to have to take care of you while I find out what's going on." He reached for me, and I growled at him. He went down on his knees, and very slowly extended his hand and stroked my head. I would've gone into my little house in the bedroom to wait for Ted, just like I always did when Ted went out alone. Instead, Milan slowly moved his hand under my belly and picked me up, and once he had me I didn't resist. He carried me out of the apartment on one arm the way Ted did, and he locked the door behind us.

Milan took me to his home in the basement. His parents, the old supers before him, were there, and his wife Jana, and his three children. Jana asked surprised, "What are you doing with Ted's dog?" When Milan told her how he found me and Ted was gone, she said, "Well, where're you going to keep it?"

"I'll take care of him," the oldest boy volunteered. "He can stay in my bedroom."

"You share your bedroom," Jana objected.

"I'll take care of him with you, Enis," the younger boy offered.

Jana looked at the two of them. "And what's to stop the dog from making a mess in your bedroom?"

"He doesn't make a mess upstairs, so why should he here?" Milan answered. "I'll get some of those pads out of Ted's apartment he keeps on the floor for him."

"And I'll walk him," Enis assured her.

"You'll have to get him some dog food, too. Are you going to do that?" Jana asked Enis.

"I'll go for some now before school," he replied. "He must be hungry." My stomach was rumbling.

Jana looked worried. "I sure hope Ted's ok. How will we find out?"

"I'll ask around the block. I'll make some calls. What else can I do?" Milan told her.

Jana looked at me again. "If Ted doesn't come back, we're going to have to do something with the dog. You'll have to call the city."

Enis made a face like he didn't like that idea, but he

said only, "I'll take care of him for Ted. And I'll take him for a walk right now and get some cans of dog food."

"Well, hurry up, or you'll be late for school." That was how Jana said, "Ok." Her voice was kind, so everything was alright. Anyway, I didn't want to live with them forever; I wanted get back with Ted. That's all that mattered.

Enis took my leash and led me through the door. I didn't dare run up the iron stairs, especially with all their empty see-through spaces, so he finally understood that he had to carry me. When he put me down on the sidewalk he said, "Don't worry. If we don't find Ted, she'll let me keep you. One step at a time."

I pulled on the leash to go back upstairs to the apartment when we passed the front entry, but Enis led me up the street instead. At least I knew these people from meeting them many times on the stoop when I went out with Ted. With them at least I was in my building. They could open all the doors I couldn't. They'd help me find Ted. I felt good about Enis as I trotted along behind him.

We rounded the corner at Sixth Avenue and went up the block to the Food Emporium. Enis dropped the loop of my leash over a parking meter and said to me, "You wait here, Tobi. Dogs can't go into grocery stores." Well, that'd never happened before. Ted always left me home when he had to go to the grocery. Here I was, outside alone again, but tied this time, so I couldn't run if I had to. I sat there trembling. What if a person came down the street with a big dog and didn't shorten his leash walking by? Ted never left me tied by myself on the street.

4. MACK

I waited nervously by the parking meter. People were coming and going. A few paused to look at me. "What a cute Chihuahua," one woman said to another. Well, I was used to that. Suddenly a tall, thin man was standing over me. He didn't smell good at all, and I jumped to my feet and growled at him. With one hand he lifted the leash loop off over the top of the parking meter; with the other he snatched me up. I fought him in his arms. I even tried to bite him, but he held me firmly, put his smelly hand over my face and held my jaws shut as he walked quickly up the street with me. When I thrashed against his grasp—and I did struggle hard and make a big fuss—he squeezed me all the tighter so I could hardly breathe. Gasping, choking, my yelping did me no good. He had me and carried me swiftly away from the grocery store. After we turned a few corners, he put me down, to pull me on my leash behind him.

I knew I was in big trouble, and I tried at first wrenching back and forth hard and fighting the leash, bracing my legs not to follow. He was strong and in a hurry, and he jerked me off my feet. He yanked me along fast, forcing me to run to keep up or be dragged, down one long block after another. Finally he turned into an entry at the side of a building and pulled me to a basement stairway so abruptly that I lost my footing and tumbled and bounced to the bottom. I sprang up, cringing from him; he gathered up my leash, drew me through a narrow passageway, then across a small courtyard to a door in the back. He opened it and hauled me inside.

There was only one small window, which made everything grey. The place had his smell. He pulled me to a shabby table and looped my leash under one of its legs. Then he opened a refrigerator and took out a bottle, and a breakfast roll from a cupboard. He ate and drank while he walked around. There was a doorway to another room, but it was too dark to see into it. I heard something move in there, and a single smell, part of everything I smelled coming into this place, got stronger. I growled and drew back when I saw a huge face in the doorway. A very big pit bull walked into the room, straight towards me. I didn't like big dogs to begin with, and this was a breed I knew always made Ted nervous. He'd tense up, shorten my leash, and say, "Over here," and he'd pull me to his side opposite the dog as we passed. Well, now here I was tied to a table, and that pit bull was on her way.

Trapped, I went completely berserk, "defensive-aggressive" Ted calls it. The hair on my shoulders bristled straight up, and I growled viciously and barked as fiercely as I could, all at the same time, and yanked at the leash rapidly one way and the other, back and forth. Unable to escape, I leaped against the leash at the dog. She stopped near the table where she towered over me. I even tried to bite her; I'd fight when there was nothing else to do. The old pit bull stood there just out of my reach, ignoring my ruckus. Instead she stared up at the man, hoping he'd share the roll with her. That interested her more than I did. It reminded me how hungry I was, too. And I was very thirsty. There was a water bowl on the floor in the corner, but tied to the table I couldn't reach it. The man didn't pay attention to either one of us. He was on his phone talking to someone.

"Victor, it's Mack. I've got a dog, a little one, a Chihuahua...."

I calmed down when the pit bull walked away from me. She stretched out by the wall near the water bowl, gave me another look, then rested her chin on the floor and sighed. I could see she was very bored. She closed her eyes and seemed to fall asleep.

"What you mean your pups aren't old enough? I don't find a dog every day. It'd be ready when they are!... No, I'm not gonna wait!... I'll sell it on the street."

When Mack got off the phone, he walked over to the kitchen corner and picked up a bag leaning against the refrigerator. He dropped a large dish down next to the water bowl and poured it full of pellets from the bag. The pit bull slowly got up and went to eat. I didn't know what the food was; I couldn't recognize the smell of it. I wondered if I was going to get any. Most of all I wanted a drink of water. Mack came over to me, reached down, and I growled at him and pulled back as far as I could under the table. He grasped the end of my leash, drew me out with it, then unhooked it. I was still in my harness, but free of the leash, so I could move around the room. Instead I rushed back under the table. He didn't seem to care what I did. He went through the dark doorway and turned on a light in the room. There was a bed, a bureau and a tall armoire for a closet. He flopped onto the bed and fell asleep.

When the pit bull finished eating, she lay back down again, this time near the bowls. She closed her eyes. I was awfully thirsty, but I didn't dare go to the water dish she blocked. Everyone was sleeping except me. Time dragged. Finally—I was so thirsty—I decided to creep carefully, tentatively, along the wall towards the water bowl. I reached it. Just then the pit bull's eye opened, but she didn't move. I froze. We looked at each other. Her look was kind, and I knew then it was ok. The water was stale, but I drank. Then I retreated as far back under the table as I could get, and I waited.

When Mack got up he grabbed a handful of pellets from the bag and dropped them into the pit bull's dish. She sighed and rose to her feet and walked towards it. Mack said, "No! Molly!" And Molly slowly turned back to the wall, lay down again, and closed her eyes with another sigh. As far under the table as I was, he shoved the dish right under my nose. The pellets had an unfamiliar, unappealing smell. The unwashed dish was rancid, and still wet with Molly's slobber. "I can't eat that," I thought, and I turned away from it. I lay down between the wall and the dish, and resting my chin on the floor, closed my eyes as Molly had done. Exhausted with misery, weak from hunger, I'd sleep, and dream of my normal breakfast of cooked chicken and warm oatmeal with milk.

It was not to be. Mack started making too much

noise on the table over me. First he dropped a carton on it, then was cutting cardboard, banging the scissors down, and rattling the drawer. Next thing, he reached down for me. Drawing back, I growled and snapped at him. He grabbed my harness and yanked me out, re-attached my leash, and then hauled me out the door. Once again he pulled me behind him so fast up the street that I had to run or be dragged.

5. WORKING THE STREET

We reached Ninth Avenue. Turning onto it, Mack pulled me along a few more blocks. Then he stopped near a street corner, where he sat down on the sidewalk with his back propped up against a building. Grabbing me again by the harness so that I couldn't bite him as I'd have liked to do, he took a string from his pocket and hung from my neck the piece of cardboard. There I sat, wearing a "For Sale" sign. If Mack expected I'd sell easily, it didn't happen. Some people looked quizzically, even amused, when they saw me, but then they walked on.

Mack also had a second, larger cardboard sign he placed on the ground in front of him, beside a paper cup; it read, "Will work for food. Dog eats first." He knew what he was doing. Setting it in place he looked at me and said, "Not to worry. Nobody will hire me because I scare 'em." And that made him chuckle. "But thinking I'm willing to work will soften 'em up." That made him laugh out loud. "And they'll help me feed the dog." It worked. He emptied the cup into his pocket regularly as passers-by dropped coins and an occasional dollar bill into it.

The late morning became noon, and the sun bore down on us. The day was stifling even in the shade. A woman stopped, reached into a grocery bag she was carrying and pulled out a small bottle of cold water she handed to Mack. "Here," she said, "I saw you on my way to the store, and I bought this for your little dog. He looks hot." Mack reached up and took the bottle without a word, not even a smile, and he set it down on the sidewalk beside him. The woman looked helplessly when she saw that he didn't give me water, and she walked on. When she was out of sight, he emptied his paper cup of coins and used it to give me a drink, and drank down the rest himself from the bottle.

The afternoon wore on. I was not so easy to sell probably because Mack looked so fierce. When an old man asked him, "Is that your dog?" he snarled back, "What do you think?" People passed by all day; most would see us then look away. Mack dozed off a couple of times. Mercifully the sun descended in the sky.

A woman approached holding onto the arm of a teenage boy. When he saw me the boy said to her, "There's a man sitting on the sidewalk with a little Chihuahua beside him. I want to take a closer look." Then he drew her nearer to us. "Can I say hello to your dog?" he asked Mack. Mack didn't care; maybe he'd buy me. "He's a beautiful little dog, Mother," the boy said to the woman who continued to look straight ahead. He extended his hand slowly towards me, and I pulled back, but I was up against the wall. He reached very slowly. I growled, but I let him softly touch the top of my head. I felt goodness through his fingertip.

"Dogs like this one, in the pet stores sell for a thousand up," Mack said to him, "so he's a bargain for a hundred dollars."

"We don't have a hundred dollars," Mother said.

"And a dog eats; you have to pay for that, too."

The boy said to me, "You're such a nice little dog."

Mack had little incentive to lower my price, because it was what he'd get from Victor if he waited, but a sale now meant money now. "What would you give me for him?" he asked the boy gruffly.

"I don't have any money," the boy answered. "I can't offer you anything."

Poor Boy rose to his feet. "He's very beautiful," he said wistfully to Mack. Then, guiding his mother, he walked on.

Mack and I sat there for a while more. Then he stood up, pocketed the last of the coins from the cup, and folded the larger sign. He left the For Sale sign around my neck, and led me up the avenue like that. Past 28th Street he tied me to a pole, entered a store, and came out carrying a tall, narrow bag. Walking fast in a really big hurry, he pulled me along again behind him. It didn't take long to get "home."

Molly was lying by the room wall exactly where we'd left her. When Mack held the door open for her, she slowly rose to her feet and went out into the alleyway where she did her business and then came back in. That's why her smell was so strong out there. Those few steps were the only walk Molly got. Mack was in a hurry. Without bothering to give her fresh water, he poured pellets into her dish. Then he pulled a bottle out of the bag, unscrewed the cap, tilted his head back, and emptied a draft of its contents down his throat. He gasped when he stopped. He walked into the bedroom and flopped onto his bed with the bottle. He hadn't thought at all about me. I had nothing to eat except any pellets Molly scattered and missed, and I ate each one now hungrily. I drank from the stale water bowl as eagerly, then went back under the table. After a while I fell asleep.

I was wakened suddenly when Mack came out of the bedroom. He staggered to the table and banged the bottle on it. He went to the refrigerator, took out some paper-wrapped cold bologna, and bread from the cabinet nearby. Swaying, he put together a sandwich, and didn't notice when he dropped a piece of the meat on the floor. Molly looked at me. "Take it," her eyes told me. I moved out cautiously, grabbed it, and ran back under the table with it. One side was covered with dust now where it hit the floor, but I gulped it down quickly. That was how I learned tramp eating. No more fussiness; just get something into my stomach whenever and however I could.

I did well to stay hidden. Mack was talking to himself, carrying on an angry conversation with someone who wasn't there. He began to yell at the person, banging the bottle on the table. I drew as far back as I could against the wall. Molly seemed used to it and didn't pay much attention.

And that's what happened, day after day, on the street, then drunk at night with the bottle I helped him buy. He said to me once, "They'll give for a dog before they'll do it for a human being. They figure I'll feed you with it. Hah!" Brooding hot days, then crazy nights, when he would rant at nobody there or at me or Molly.

"You're my bottle of liquor, baby," he told me blubbering one evening, then sobbing. Through his tears he said to me, "I never did so good without you out there, Pipsqueak. I'm going to name you Whiskey." But he never did; it was always Pipsqueak.

By now Molly was leaving more pellets for me. When she saw me licking up her leftovers, she understood that one dish had to do for both of us. I supplemented that diet with what I sometimes found in the street as Mack dragged me along, an occasional pizza remnant by a trash can or remains of rice and beans in an open Styrofoam container abandoned on a stoop. If I spotted something and pulled towards it, Mack might slow down enough to let me eat it. I spent most days without water in the sun. Mack and I sat in the rain, too. "Rain is good—it makes people pity, good for the cup," Mack said, talking to himself. And I could lick water from the crevices in the sidewalk. I never used to like walking out in the rain, but now I welcomed it. I was toughening.

I also was becoming thinner and more haggard. That affected the cup, and not for the better. People took more pity on a cute dog than a starving, ragged one. One evening when Mack could afford only a small bottle, but got just as drunk, he said to me, "I'm going to sell you, Pipsqueak. I'll use Molly out there; I don't need you."

Molly and I were friends now very simply. Sometimes I slept beside her. She occasionally licked me.

6. MADNESS

Some evenings, instead of starting to drink right away, Mack would make a sandwich and take a short nap. When he awoke those times, he always was very tense. He'd hurry around the place, take things out of a drawer, and then go out.

He'd come back with other things he'd put on the table. Not long later there'd be a knock at the door, and a hooded man would give Mack something and take the things on the table. It was done quickly. They hardly spoke, and the man was gone. Mack would go to the bedroom and lie back on the bed, his eyes open. Then he'd get really crazy.

I'd been living with Mack and Molly for a while when he went totally insane one night that way. He staggered out of the bedroom laughing. "Come here, Bait!" It was as if calling me Bait was the funniest idea he'd ever had. I hurried under the table. Mack's face changed to surprise to anger. His jaw was chewing and chewing, even though he wasn't eating anything. Then he started to laugh again. "When Victor gets you, he'll take you down a peg. Ha, ha, ha."

As Mack moved towards me, he tripped over Molly. He must've hurt her, because she growled and bared her teeth at him. He got to his hands and knees and crawled very fast after me under the table. I pulled as far back as I possibly could, but I was trapped. I growled, and I snapped at his hand flying at me. It grabbed me hard. I screamed and fought to get free, but he had me by the neck, and he pulled me out. Still kneeling, he held me up at arm's length. "Ha, ha, ha. Bait! Ha, ha, ha." I was choking and thrashing. Molly retreated to the bedroom, then looked out from there to see what was happening.

Kicking, I scratched Mack's arm deeply with the nails of my back feet. His eyes popped as his face kept chewing. "Ow-w-w!" he yelled and dropped me. I ran back under the table—there was nowhere else to go. Right away Mack was on his hands and knees after me. He grasped for me again. I bit him hard, so he yanked back. Molly was watching. Then he crawled at me again very fast, grabbed me, this time with both hands, bumping his head hard on the bottom of the table doing it. He was choking me, so I went berserk, but the way he was holding me I couldn't reach him. He crawled out on elbows and knees, then stood up with me. His face was twisting and chewing terribly. He snarled, "Bite me, you dirty rat, I'll kill you!" and he threw me against the wall. I hit it with a terrible thud that smashed through me, and I fell hard to the floor. I couldn't move because the room was turning. I was going into and out of blackness. I struggled against it; I needed to see to get away from him.

Molly had walked into the room again, and Mack backed into her. He turned and kicked her to one side. She fell, then got up. She shook herself, as if to clear her head. He started to lurch back at me, but she stopped him cold with a loud bark. He looked at her, and she bared her teeth. Molly moved very slowly towards him, crouching as if to spring. Mack came to his senses enough to realize the danger he was in. He yelled at her, "Back, Molly!" But she kept coming, stalking him. He kicked at her, and his foot just missed her head. He kicked at her again, and she grabbed his pants leg. Mack yanked back, tearing the cloth in her teeth. He ran into the bedroom, but she bounded right behind him. He jumped up on the bureau, and then up onto the top of the armoire. Leaning on the furniture with her forepaws, Molly stood on her hind legs, snarling, trying to reach him. He couldn't even let his legs hang over. He sat cross-legged up there in the small space. Molly sat at the bottom, looking up at him, daring him to come down.

With everything stopped by Molly, I began to catch my breath, and my wits returned. I dragged myself back under the table. My body ached everywhere, and I licked wherever I could reach that hurt the most.

Barking, snarling, a person screaming, was a lot of noise in the middle of the night. People yelled across the courtyard to be quiet, and that they were "going to call the cops." Although our house had grown still now with Mack and Molly waiting each other out, there eventually was a loud knock at the door. Mack didn't want anybody to come in. He yelled, "Go away! Go away! Go away!" Molly came and barked at the door like she was supposed to do, which started the noise again for the officers. They opened the door. Mack yelled down from the armoire, "Quiet, Molly!" and she lay down by the wall as docile as any pet could be, no threat at all anymore. Mack for his part was too out of his mind to explain what he was doing on top of the furniture, or to answer anything else coherently. The officers went to help him down.

"You'd better come with us," one told him.

"Think we ought to call an ambulance?" the other asked his partner.

I scooted out the open door. They never saw me.

Getting up the iron stairs was painfully hard. Once on the street I began to hobble away. I didn't know where I was going; I never knew where I was anymore anyway. I just walked, to get as far from Mack as I could. When I turned onto an avenue, I felt I was heading towards the Village. I couldn't run; I hurt too much. I stopped for cars at each street crossing the way Ted taught me, but at that hour there wasn't much traffic. The few people on the avenue were walking quickly to wherever they had to go. I avoided any hangers-out I saw.

It was early fall by then; days were still warm, but nights were growing cooler. Adding to the knocks I'd just taken, I increasingly felt the chill; and as I continued on, it penetrated my aches more and more. Soon I was shivering so much that it was difficult to keep my balance. As much as I could only think of stopping and curling up somewhere warm, there was no place to do that, no place warm and hidden. At the same time I wanted to put distance between me and Mack. I thought warm thoughts, of my fleece-lined little house at home with Ted, of falling asleep on that luxurious softness. And that's the way I limped along through Chelsea towards the Village.

The darkness in which I trekked eventually began to give way to a thin line of light that expanded over the building tops. Dawn was breaking. More people appeared on the avenue. I'd been walking for a long time, so I sensed myself well away from Mack. I had to find a place to rest. I had to get warm. I had to lick my hurts. Eventually, at long last, I came upon a narrow, partially covered alleyway that was deep and dark, so I could barely see the back wall, but there seemed to be a bunch of rags and bags piled back there. I figured I could crawl into that. I'd be hidden and warm; I could finally rest, and probably do what my body yearned for, sleep.

7. AGNES

I approached the heap carefully. Closer, I could see that it really consisted of several stuffed garbage bags standing guard around a bed of coats and blankets. I nudged my nose under one corner, and the whole pile stirred. I jumped back; there was someone under it. I ran out of the alleyway; this wasn't a safe place. But when I stood in the mounting daylight in the street again, I realized that wasn't an option now, either. What to do?

I didn't have much choice, because I'd seen no other shelter and I didn't want to collapse on the street. The person obviously was asleep, so wouldn't try to hurt me for now. I could crawl very quietly under an edge of the pile, and there rest and warm up. I'd stay awake and run when I had to. So that's what I did. After hesitating, I went back to the heap.

My body hurt, but my chill slowly subsided. My little nest under the corner of the blankets grew warmer and warmer from my own body heat; and in the comfort of it, exhausted, I fell asleep. I didn't waken until I felt a weight of blankets fall on top of me. The person, getting up, had thrown them back over me. What to do? I braced myself to jump out, but I was buried and not sure now which way was out. As I pushed one way and then the other under the blanket, a woman's voice up over me began to cry out in alarm. I was scared of her, and she was scared of me. When I finally found the way to poke my head out of the blanket, I stared up at an old lady, and she stared back at me.

"Well, where'd you come from?" she asked me.

What to do? I was about to leap out from the blanket. I'd dash out of the alleyway. If I did it fast enough, she couldn't catch me.

"What's your name, Sweetheart?" she asked me. "Sweetheart" was a magic word right then, a warm and loving name Ted often called me. I hesitated, watching her carefully. She said to me, "My name is Agnes. What's yours, Sweetheart?"

I'd have answered, "Sweetheart," if I could have. It made me feel good; it sounded like home. It told me that I probably didn't have to worry about this person. She seemed caring. She didn't try to reach her hand out towards me like other strangers often did; she must've known that would threaten me, and I'd be gone in an instant. She just kept talking to me while she made her bed and rearranged her things.

"Where'd you come from?" she asked me again. Then she answered for me what she surmised, "Somebody must've dropped you off. That's what people do when they don't want dogs anymore; they just drop them off. That is what happened to you. You were dropped off."

Agnes untied the knot at the top of one of the stuffed garbage bags and opened it, and took out several articles of clothing. "Well, what should I wear today?" she asked. She was asking herself, not me. That's one thing I learned about Agnes. It was hard sometimes to know whether she was talking to me or to herself.

Once she'd chosen a blue dress from the array, as well as a pink sweater, and—yes—undergarments and stockings, she put back the rest she'd taken out, and re-knotted the top of the bag carefully. Then she took the items she'd selected and stuffed them into a flight bag. I heard her toothbrush and comb rattle in the bottom of it. She slung the bag over her shoulder and began to walk out of the alleyway.

I was going to stay back and crawl beneath the warm blankets again. When she saw me hesitate, she said to me, "C'mon, let's go, c'mon." I was hungry; maybe there would be some breakfast. So I decided to trot after her.

The street we followed opened on Hudson River Park. Agnes headed straight for a small building that had the word WOMEN over the door. She disappeared inside, leaving me standing there. I decided to wait. I still thought I smelled food inside her flight bag. When she came out, she looked refreshed. She was wearing the blue dress and the pink sweater, and white ankle socks over stockings.

"Hello, there!" she said to me, as if we were meeting for the first time. She walked a little way up the park, which was still almost empty of people, except for a few running along the esplanade like Ted and I used to do mornings. Agnes chose a bench facing out across the river and sat down. She opened the flight bag and took out a huge muffin. That certainly got my attention. I stood at her feet wagging my tail; I wanted some of that.

Agnes took a paper napkin, spread it on her lap, and

unwrapped the muffin upon it. It smelled good, and I was really interested now. She broke a piece of it off and held it down to me. I took it. She broke off another piece, so daintily, and ate it herself. Then it was my turn; she gave me a second piece, and then another for herself; then a third for me, and another for herself. That's how we ate it. I gulped each piece down fast to be ready for the next one, but Agnes ate slowly like she wanted to enjoy that muffin forever. She was in no hurry at all. While we ate she looked out across the river, or down at me as she shared with me, and in her eyes and her smile I could see she was happy. Then Agnes took a small cup from her flight bag and walked over to a water fountain close by. Filling it, she took a drink, then did the same for me. This was the best attention I'd gotten since losing Ted. When she finished with the cup, she rinsed it and put it back into her bag. We returned to the bench facing the river.

Agnes sat quietly looking across the Hudson to the New Jersey shore lined with tall buildings that were radiant now in blue and burgundy and grey reflecting the sun rising behind us. She sighed with satisfaction. When she reached down to me, I let her stroke my head. Then I let her tickle my stomach. Eventually she had me up on the bench with her. Then she nestled me on her lap. I usually don't accept someone that fast, but I got very good feelings from Agnes. Besides, she'd given me some of her muffin. The early morning was chilly, and sitting still I began to shiver. Agnes opened her sweater, drew me near and wrapped one side of it over me like a blanket. It felt very good. With my body covered now, and my head warmed by the rising sun, I was close to falling asleep. She continued to gaze across the river, sighing from time to time—not an unhappy sigh, but a long contented one. "It's so-o-o beautiful," she said to me, or to herself. We sat there for a long while, that first morning, Agnes and I.

Eventually, Agnes put me down and stood up. We walked along the park, northward, as it follows the river's shore. I could tell that she was not going anywhere in particular. She just was enjoying the day. I walked beside her, enjoying the day, too. At least as well as I could with my limp and soreness, which took some time to heal.

8. ON LEASH AGAIN WITH MANY HOMES

Agnes and I became friends, close friends. Every day followed a pattern. That's what I liked. Never any surprises. Just a steady flow of things I could count on. I guess our day began really at night, late evening, after a nap. We'd set out from our alleyway just as the grocery stores were closing, when Agnes could go through the containers they put out for the garbage trucks.

Agnes knew all the stores, and exactly what time she should show up. She filled her shopping bags with such good things, muffins and breads and cookies, and cereal flakes, too. There were things only she'd eat, like ripe bananas, and apples, and carrots still in their packets, and lettuce she ate one leaf at a time. There were things she picked up just for me when she figured out what I'd eat, like butcher scraps and packages of meat. They were fine raw for me, but Agnes wouldn't eat them that way. One night we found a whole box of vanilla pudding cups; I love vanilla. We didn't eat where we found the food; we took it all home in Agnes' shopping bags, two of them, so loaded that she waddled as she carried them. Back at our alley we'd have dinner. Then Agnes would store the rest in one of her big, black plastic garbage bags. The next morning she'd put enough in her flight bag to keep us for our breakfast and lunch and treats while we wandered about during the day.

Mornings were like the first one I experienced with her, always somewhere along Hudson River Park on nice days. We sat on the benches, then walked a bit, then sat for a while more. I'd often fall asleep on her lap. Sometimes, sitting there in the sun she'd doze off, too. Around noontime if we went back to the alley, Agnes would check through all her bags to find out what was missing. "The kids from the playground have been into my bags again," she'd invariably say. I never saw any kids, and there wasn't a playground anywhere nearby. She always concluded, "Well, no one took anything this time." Afterwards she'd "make lunch," taking out food we'd gleaned the night before, and after a nap when I snuggled close to her, we'd wander the streets some more. Agnes liked to look into the store windows. "Let's go shopping," she'd say.

I'd walk along behind Agnes having a good time for myself, sniffing here and there, easily distracted, but always looking up in time to run to catch up with her. Then one day she was stopped by a woman, a very cranky woman, who told her, "You're not supposed to have a dog off-leash in New York City. The policemen will take it away from you."

"Oh, my," Agnes, very concerned, answered her.

I was still wearing my harness. It hadn't been off me since Ted's accident, but my leash had stayed back at Mack's. Agnes looked around, spotted a piece of twine in one of the street-corner trash cans, and tied it to my harness. It'd been more fun to be free, but I felt comfortable back on leash, too. It was a safety link with my person. I'd always stopped in my tracks when Ted dropped ours, waiting for him to pick it up. Now Agnes and I were a happy pair, too, leash-connected.

It also made crossing streets easier; Agnes would watch for the cars as Ted used to do—I didn't have to think about them. But I still watched out; sometimes when a car was coming that I thought Agnes didn't see, I pulled her back. She usually didn't agree with me though. She'd say, "We're crossing legally, Precious, and in New York a car has to stop for a person crossing legally." I'd no way of knowing the difference. If a car was coming, I ducked.

That day I was Precious, but Agnes changed our names a lot; it was one of her favorite "pretend" games. She'd be Lily and I'd be Honey Sweet, and then another day we'd be Deborah and Sugar, or Vanessa and Prince. But most of the time she was Agnes and I was Precious. She never thought up my name Tobi Little Deer. Agnes probably really was her name because that's what her friend Mathilde called her.

Over time I learned that our alley wasn't Agnes' only home. She had two more she used when we wandered farther up Hudson River Park. One was inside a shed beneath a bridge where buses traveled overhead. In one corner was a grate where heat came up into the shack from the ground, so it became more comfortable than our alleyway as the season grew colder. Agnes arranged the interior pretty much the same with blankets and coats for a bed, but with fewer stuffed garbage bags standing about, because there was less room. However, going there made me nervous. The surrounding streets were dark caverns between high black buildings. I sensed we weren't far from Mack.

The third home, my favorite with a real bed, was still farther north; we'd go there to visit Mathilde. Usually, as we walked up Hudson River Park we'd encounter her standing by a railing above the river, holding her broad hat on her head with one hand. I think she stood there for hours, because it was always the same. With the same greeting, "*Chère* Ang-yes."

The two women were not alike at all. Whereas Agnes was short, a little stubby person, Mathilde was tall, skinny, bony, and her narrow face with its hooked nose looked like that of an old hawk. Agnes' clothing was different each day, but Mathilde always wore the same slim, ankle-length, yellowed lace dress. When we went out shopping, she added a tattered fox fur and her broad-brimmed ribboned hat. It never changed.

We never stayed with Mathilde very long—usually just a night or two. But it was a real apartment in a building with an elevator, and a terrace overlooking the Hudson River, and Agnes and I slept in our own room. The doorman spoke nicely to us when we came and went. He'd telephone, "Miss Agnes is back." And he'd say to Agnes, "Go ahead up." He'd hold the door whenever he saw Mathilde, and she'd always say, "The young man, he resembles Jean-Luc."

When we arrived, Mathilde would give Agnes a big hug and make tea. She'd call her "*Chère* Ang-yes," and "*Ma chérie*." She always called me "Fee-fee," and when we were with Mathilde, Agnes called me Fee-Fee, too. They'd sit, and Mathilde would talk.

All the furniture in the apartment was very old. Sometimes Mathilde took out a feather duster and started tidying it up. "I'm expecting Jean-Luc," she'd explain. Whenever she said that, it meant we couldn't stay the night.

Eventually, we always returned to our alley home in Chelsea. It was our main one.

9. HEARTBREAK

One day we wandered still farther south to the Village. It felt good to go back. Everything was so familiar, just like I'd left it. I was on the twine leash, but Agnes followed where I led her. We came down Seventh Avenue, took a left onto Waverly Place, and passed the spot where the accident had happened. Agnes let me sniff, but there was no scent of Ted. I led her around the corner, and we walked to the building where I lived. When we reached it, I surprised Agnes by running up the steps and standing on the landing in front of the door. The leash was just long enough. I looked at her as eagerly as I could, wagging my tail. I wanted to go inside to find Ted and be back home.

Agnes seemed to understand. "Is this where you live?" she asked me. "Is that why you were pulling me down the street?" She thought for a moment, like she didn't know what to do; then she suggested, "I'll show you where I live!" With the leash she drew me down the steps and led me the short distance to Greenwich Avenue, where I looked back just as she was taking me around the corner.

I saw Ted quickly appear on the landing, descend the steps, and turn in the opposite direction. I put on the brakes, tried to stop; I barked, "Here I am! See me! See me!" However, Agnes had taken me out of sight. "Why didn't he see me?" I whined, and then I barked for Agnes to stop and let me run after him. When she didn't, I fought against the leash, struggled to pull her back, wrenched from side to side to escape and braced my legs not to follow; but she wanted to go where she was headed, and that was that, and she held me fast. "I don't know what's wrong with Precious today," she protested to passers-by who were giving her looks at the sight of my ruckus. Agnes was on a mission now as she hauled me up the avenue. "What is wrong with you, Precious?" she asked impatiently, pulling me along, until she spotted the school yard across the street. As if by afterthought, she towed me over to it.

Children were playing behind the high double-fence, very little ones. A few were trying to throw hoops with a basketball, like big boys, but most were gathered in circular games with their teachers. Whatever they did, they all screamed very loud.

Agnes stood in front of the locked gate looking in, while I waited beside her. I wanted to get back to Ted; so nudging her ankle with my nose, I looked up at her to move on. But she was staring, thinking very deeply, with a tear running down her face. "Precious, this is where I was a teacher," she said, "first grade, for a long time. So long that I'd even taught their mothers and fathers. So many years..." Her voice drifted off, and she stood silent. She remained a while looking in, watching the children. When I pulled on the leash, she ignored me.

Agnes finally turned and led me up the street. "You showed me where you live, and I'm going to show you where I do." She took me across Seventh Avenue at West 11ᵗʰ Street and pointed to windows close to the top of the "Two Boots" building there. "That's where, Precious. That's where my beautiful things are. See the sunshine on the windows?—perfect for my plants. Before I retired, I'd come home there every day after school. I'd turn on music, and make dinner, and correct papers or watch television, and my apartment was full of music. If I didn't watch television, sometimes I'd have friends over, or we'd go to the theater, because I had so many good friends, Precious, teachers, like me, from my school; they'd stop by." Agnes hesitated, and then added sadly, "But time marches on; you never know what's going to happen, you just never know." She was standing right beside me, but her voice began to sound like she was far away.

Agnes' words became so soft and low and slow I'm not sure she really was talking to me anymore. "I raised my boy and girl there, Precious. I did it all by myself, because their daddy was a fireman and he was killed when they were just babies. My little boy and my little girl were so-o-o beautiful growing up, and both so-o smart. I know, I had them in my class at school. I was so proud of them; 'so lucky,' that's what I'd say to myself, and that's what people said to me."

As she continued, it was like Agnes was recounting a story she'd repeated many times, over and over, and she sounded very tired when she had to tell it all again. "Priscilla was the quieter one; but Mack, he was out there doing everything! Baseball and basketball, and football, I'd go to his games. He was heading for college, to become a doctor." Agnes' face showed her thinking very hard; then she said looking down at me, "But things don't happen like you plan, Precious." I wagged my tail, I wanted to go.

Agnes looked up at her home again with a long, very weary sigh. "They went out with their friends, and they both met trouble. Different kinds of trouble, but trouble is trouble. Priscilla had a beautiful little baby named Elsa. I told her she didn't have to marry the guy, but she did, and they went away. Mack stayed around, somewhere around here . . . I never knew where. . . ." Agnes collected her thoughts, seemed unsure, then said with resentment, "He'd scare me when he came back. And I'd say, 'Mack, don't make me cry,' and he'd take my things and walk out the door with them in plain sight."

Agnes hesitated again, as if afraid to endure the memory. I wagged my tail to move on—I'd seen Ted. "Priscilla . . . my Priscilla came back to the building one day, and she went up to the roof without even stopping to say hello and flew up to heaven." Agnes paused, and she asked me, "Why?" I could see her tears. I wagged my tail, impatient to get going. Then, still very thoughtfully, she told me what happened afterwards. "My home became too, too sad, too many memories, good and bad, too much to think about, for me alone in there. So I decided to take a walk. And here we are, you and me." She added with another sigh, "Someday I'll figure it all out. Someday I'll probably go back home. But not quite yet, Precious." Agnes put her hand to her face and sniffled, and then with a look of relief at having finished, she showed me a smile.

"Let's go sit by the river," she said.

Agnes walked quickly, as if she couldn't reach Hudson Park fast enough. I tried to look back when I could, but Ted was nowhere to be seen. At the river's edge, Agnes sat on one of the benches, took me onto her lap and looked across the water at the view, like we did mornings. She gave a big, satisfied sigh. We stayed quiet a long time, and I fell asleep in the sun.

10. HAPPILY WITH AGNES

Agnes was almost never sad, however. She usually was just very simply happy. And she was happiest out and about in the city, which was most of the time, among the people hurrying by. Sometimes we walked north to Times Square where she led me up and down and back and forth. Suddenly she'd stop, and take a deep breath, and with a smile give a sweet sigh. She'd reach her arms out to the excitement she felt beneath the towering signs, and say things like, "We're standing outside, Precious, with the city shining all over us." At night the oscillating colors that lit the place like daylight made her clap her hands. She'd say, "I love it here." Agnes was so happy in Times Square. It didn't make much difference to me, except when she didn't watch where she was going and stepped on my foot, and I yelped, which made everyone look at us.

Afternoons in good weather, we shopped the store windows beneath the midtown skyscrapers or made our way through the crowds up and down the mall stores in the grand old buildings that line Sixth Avenue. They were the closest ones to where our alleyway was on the far west side of Chelsea. Sometimes we'd venture carefully into one of them. A security officer told Agnes she had to carry me. "His feet can't touch the floor," the man said.

"Why is that?" Agnes questioned, although not loud enough for him to hear. "Precious is cleaner than most people." At the time that was not saying much for "most people." I hadn't had a bath since Ted. But Agnes did as she was told. Holding me kept her hands occupied, too, so she wasn't scolded in that store for handling the merchandise.

Afternoons on especially sunny days Agnes liked to lead me on my twine leash up and down Eighth Avenue in Chelsea with all its sidewalk cafés and colorful shop windows. I could tell she thought we looked pretty smart. People used to stop Ted on the street all the time to admire me, but no one was stopping us now. Agnes didn't look too bad; she changed her clothes every day. Either she found new ones, or she washed them in the park bathroom and spread them on a bench to dry. She'd go back later to get them if they were still there. People stared at her for her clothing combinations, not because she was dirty. But she didn't bathe me, so I was pretty scruffy. No, nobody admired us, and they didn't come too close.

Agnes liked late afternoons best for these Eighth Avenue walks. We'd progress slowly as she took in the sights. She'd observe the people sitting at restaurant tables lining the sidewalk, and quickly look away when they noticed her. "Mustn't stare," she'd say to me. We kept going; she didn't bother anyone. We caught their eyes because we were unusual, but Agnes was alright living just beyond everyone like that. She was satisfied to share from the curb. She wasn't thinking she was outside it all. Whenever she tired, she'd find a stoop where we could sit for a while. Then she'd take me on her lap, and it was our turn to watch the passers-by.

Sometimes these walks reached the posh stores and the chic cafés at the west end of Fourteenth Street, but Agnes didn't care for those so much, though. I could sense the way she pulled me close with the twine leash that they made her uneasy. Eventually she'd say, "These people are giving us bad looks, Precious," and we'd turn back.

More frequently we ended up in the quainter West Village, old and pleasant, where we'd both lived. Agnes always found tiny McCarthy Square on Seventh Avenue totally charming, so it was one of her favorite destinations. A small triangle of flowers and bushes, with benches surrounding a statue and a towering flag pole, it was the perfect place to stop, rest, and spend lots of time. From a safe bench in the little park we could enjoy the happy scene at the sidewalk-restaurant tables across the narrow street.

I was all attention in McCarthy Square. It's right around the block from where I lived with Ted, and he used to take me across it every day on our walks; so I had good reason to hope he'd pass by while I sat there an hour or more with Agnes. I watched expectantly to see whether he might appear on Waverly or else come across Seventh Avenue on Charles, all the streets that converged there, and he'd discover me with Agnes. I liked Agnes a lot; we were companions in the storm. Life was a lot easier with Ted, though, and I was still bonded with him, in my memory at least. I knew that Ted was back home; I remembered seeing him come out of our building that day right after I'd just walked by there with Agnes. Every time, though, Ted never showed up. And I regretfully, yes disappointedly, followed Agnes, my feet and heart dragging, back up into Chelsea, back to our alleyway, each time. So close yet so far; it tore me apart. I wanted to be back home.

11. JENNY

Month after month passed with Agnes. The weather grew cool, and all the leaves fell; then it got colder. Sometimes it snowed, which I enjoyed until the melt mixed with salt on the sidewalks and burned my feet; so back on our blankets I tried to lick it off. Later we began to see tiny new lights everywhere in the streets and windows, and all over the tree branches. It was at that time, when Agnes had decorated her bags and blankets with bits of ribbon, that we came upon Jenny and Charlie.

We found them on a cold, damp, dreary day when we'd been wandering through the Village, and we were on our way back to our alley I hoped. Walking slowly with Agnes had me thoroughly chilled. She was wearing a coat, but I didn't have one yet because dog clothes turn up very rarely in the trash. She'd tried an old shirt on me, but that hadn't worked because I tripped in it and didn't like it at all. So I was outside with her with my back hunched and shaking uncontrollably. All I could think of was the warm blankets in our alley, and I would have run straight back there at full gallop by myself if Agnes hadn't had me on the twine leash. The best I could do was try to pull her along; that effort warmed me a little.

Large snowflakes began to fall as we turned north up Sixth Avenue. Nearly at the corner of Fourteenth Street, I saw a big white dog, a boxer-type, lying placidly on a piece of cardboard on the sidewalk beside a young man who was sitting cross-legged, his back against the building. The dog, her short white fur soiled grey, wore a very dirty matching white jacket, and I wished I had one, too. With her head resting on her forepaws and her eyes closed, she didn't even notice me. The boy was exceptionally dirty, face, hands, clothes, like he'd just stepped out of a coal bin. He had an army blanket draped over his head and shoulders, reminiscent of a young sage, that partly covered the dog, too. A paper cup was set on the sidewalk in front of them, but neither was paying any attention to the passersby. The boy was engrossed in a ragged paperback resting on his lap, while the white dog slept. I gave her a yap as we passed, but she didn't look up.

Around the corner just a few feet farther, we encountered another person sitting similarly on the sidewalk, her back to the building, but without coat or blanket, a young woman, a girl really, in only a flimsy dress, trying to nurse a very tiny baby. The baby had a little blanket wrapped around him, but both were shivering. Agnes had not paid any attention to the boy, but now she did a double take. "Jenny, oh Jenny," she said very concerned, and the girl looked up.

"You need a coat, Jenny," Agnes told her. "Come with me; I'll give you one."

"I can't. I need money for food," Jenny answered.

"I have food. Come with me, I have food," Agnes told her, as she reached for the girl's arm and began to lift her to her feet.

Jenny was trembling so badly, with snowflakes

landing upon her now, that she was easily persuaded. We turned west down Fourteenth Street the three of us, Agnes holding Jenny's arm, Jenny shivering as she clutched her little baby, and me shaking at the end of the twine leash. Our alley was more than two long avenue blocks away, and it seemed to take forever to get there in the increasing snowfall. I became aware that far behind us, following us, was the boy, wrapped in his blanket, and the white dog.

Once in our alleyway, Agnes enveloped Jenny with her baby in blankets so they'd get warm. Then Agnes took food from one of her bags, breads and packages of cupcakes and bananas and stale crackers and cheese after she broke off the mold. I hopped excitedly when I saw the cheese, and she gave me a piece. Jenny didn't want much besides the sealed cupcakes and a banana. Gradually, as she ate wrapped in blankets, her shivering stopped, and her baby enveloped in warmth now began to get his color back, too. Agnes offered her some sealed cups of vanilla pudding, my favorite, so I hopped persuasively again; but Agnes' attention was on Jenny, not me, so I didn't get any. Agnes also offered her a bottle of water she'd filled at a Hudson River Park fountain that morning.

While Jenny sat against the alley wall upon Agnes' blankets, with blankets wrapped over her shoulders and over her head and around her body, she held the little baby close to her chest, and he began sucking like a puppy. "Look at Charlie," she said to Agnes, "he's feeling better already; he's hungry." I'd never seen such a little person before. Watching him was quite fascinating. Together the mother and baby looked like a big picture Agnes had stopped to look at in front of a church we'd been walking by that morning. Agnes had gazed at it tenderly and given one of her sighs, and then with the tips of her fingers touched her forehead, and then touched one shoulder and then the other, while she moved her lips.

As Jenny ate her second cupcake and second cup of pudding, and I wagged my tail for more cheese, Agnes opened another bag. She took clothing from it, all clean and neatly folded, which she spread out for Jenny to choose. Then Agnes, too, sat on the blankets her back against the wall, gazing blissfully at Jenny and Charlie. She began to sing softly, "*Away in a manger, no crib for His bed, the little Lord Jesus lay down his sweet head,...*" while Jenny looked back at her and laughed because Agnes was being so amusing.

When Charlie fell asleep, Jenny rose, set him on the blankets, wrapped him in more blankets, and she and Agnes turned their attention to the clothing. Most of it was too big for Jenny, but a sweater and a coat fit her well enough that she put them on. While they were busy, all my attention was on Charlie. I could see his face sticking out of the blanket, and I went over to investigate him. I touched his cheek with my nose and he squeaked like my toys did back home. So I poked him with my nose again, just like I used to do my squishy toy balls, and he squeaked again. I liked Jenny's little person, and I began to lick his face.

Jenny yelled and threw the coat in her hand, landing it on top of me and Charlie who started crying little shrieks. I scurried out from under it as fast as I could, just in time to catch a blow on my head from a boot Agnes hurled at me. "Stay away, Precious," Agnes said to me firmly. The boot hit me squarely, a sharp pain in my face, and the alleyway began to tilt. I closed my eyes, rubbed the hurt with my paw, and then did my best to slink farther away. The alley wall was as far as I could go, so with my ears back, I slowly, cautiously, crept along it, my eyes watching Jenny and Agnes to make sure nothing more was flying in my direction. I stopped at the alley entrance, where I lay down, a safe distance, to rub my face. I'd been a very bad dog without realizing it, which is how that usually happens. I knew now it was important to stay away from Charlie; getting close to him was being very bad. I'd made my friend Agnes angry, and I had to keep away from her, too, until she forgave me.

Jenny sat Charlie up against the wall, and she and Agnes continued to look at the clothing—until he tipped over. Then Jenny sat down again in the blankets to hold him in her arms, with blankets wrapped around them both. Agnes settled just across, cooing at Charlie, talking babyish to him like she did to me sometime, and then she started to sing again, "*Away in a manger,...*" and Jenny laughed again at her singing. No one paid any attention to the bad dog. I laid my head on my forepaws with my ears back, looked at them and wagged the tip of my tail just a bit against the floor, but nobody noticed me. They left me crying silently there all alone.

When she finished singing, Agnes said, "I have another home, a heated one under the bridges; we could go there. Charlie would never be cold. Heat comes out of the ground."

"I have to do better for him," Jenny answered.

"Why don't you live with Mathilde, then?" Agnes ventured. "She has lots of room."

"Granny? Why would she care? She's too weird," and Jenny shuddered. "I'll do better than that, too."

"Where, child, where?" Agnes asked her. "Give Mathilde a chance to help. Go see your Granny. My heart cries every day because my sweet daughter didn't stop to see me."

Later, still feeling my hurt, but shivering uncontrollably without covers, I crawled closer to Agnes' blankets, to the nearest corner, the farthest from Jenny and Charlie, raised the edge with my nose and crawled under, where safer and warmer, I eventually fell asleep.

12. THE WHITE DOG — AND COMPANY

The storm continued through the night and most of the next day. I stayed beneath the edge of the blankets, away from Jenny and Charlie and Agnes. When I got thirsty I went out to the entry with my tail between my legs and ate some snow. Agnes still didn't pay any attention to me; all she looked at was Charlie. And she cooed and cooed at him, even when he was napping. It was a very long day.

Late evening as the weather cleared, three figures appeared at the entry, silhouetted in the last grey of twilight. I jumped up and barked; Agnes, startled seeing them, went quiet. It was the white dog and the boy, with another boy.

The one we'd seen on the street peered into the darkness and called out, "Jenny?"

"What do you want, Peter?" Jenny's voice answered him from the back of the alley. "Go away."

Peter flipped on a flashlight and shone it on Agnes and Jenny. Agnes held up her hand to shade her eyes from the blinding light. I was so surprised I stopped barking and retreated farther from them. For the moment I forgot my hurt.

"Andy and I are playing, Jenny; come play with us," Peter said.

"No," Jenny answered flatly, "Not with Charlie."

"Please tell them to go away," Agnes whispered to Jenny.

"Go away," Jenny repeated once more.

Instead, the two boys sat themselves just inside the alley entrance, wrapped in Peter's blanket, and settled to wait. I barked a couple more times, but the white dog was so placid that I quieted, not sure what to do. I didn't want to be around them, but I was still exiled from Agnes, so I, too, lay down to wait—and watch, by the wall midway between the two parties. Peter kept turning on his flashlight and shining it all around the alley, including frequently on Agnes and Jenny. I could tell that Agnes was getting very annoyed. "Please ask them to leave," she insisted out loud. "Who are they?"

"Peter is Charlie's daddy," Jenny answered her, as if that were reason enough.

Peter kept playing with the light, bobbing it on the alley walls, laughing from time to time with Andy. We never had such goings-on in our alley; Agnes and I were always quiet, and when it was dark, it was dark, so no one ever noticed us there. The boys and the bobbing light and little Charlie crying and Jenny, and Agnes' agitation I could sense, all made me lie there head and ears erect, waiting expectantly for whatever.

A stranger appeared in the entrance, attracted undoubtedly by the bobbing light. Agnes called out, "Mack, is that you?" As if I were not shivering enough from cold outside the blankets, that made me really shake. The night was just getting weirder. Why did Agnes say that, to scare the boys? Then I thought I did see Mack far outside standing in a shadow, and my shoulder hair bristled. The flashlight illumined all of Agnes' things she'd set out for Jenny. The stranger looked in at them, and at all of us, then walked away. Mack was gone, too. Trembling, I returned to the edge of the blankets and burrowed under.

Peter and Andy left during the night, but they appeared again in the morning as Agnes was tidying up and Jenny was nursing Charlie. "Come on with us," they called to Jenny from the entry. "Come and play!" Jenny must already have thought about it because she was ready. She'd gotten over whatever Peter had done to annoy her the previous day, because, wearing a coat Agnes had given her, and with tiny Charlie cupped in her arms, she walked out to join them, giving Agnes no other explanation except, "I want to go now. Thank you, Agnes."

Agnes stood there watching her depart. Then she looked at me and said, "Just because we want to help, Precious, doesn't mean we can."

Agnes reached down and tickled me behind my ears. She appeared to be my friend again; but it took me a little while to be sure. As she patted me I put my belly to the ground, with my ears back, to let her know I knew I'd been bad, and that I wasn't sure yet if everything was alright. I kept a distance, slinking along by the edge of the blanket until Agnes offered me some vanilla pudding, which reassured me that everything was back to normal between us. But from then on, I'd always have eyes in the back of my head to see if she was throwing something.

A few weeks later, after the little lights everywhere

disappeared and Agnes had removed the ribbons from her bags, we were crossing a street just south of Cooper Square when we encountered Jenny and the two boys walking towards us through the intersection. Laughing hilariously, as if at some wonderful joke one had told, the boys seemed unsure of their footing; Jenny acted happy, too, but was walking better than they. The iconic white dog clung to Peter. Jenny looked better than the two boys; she must have washed somewhere they didn't. She smiled a hello to Agnes as they were passing.

Agnes put her hand out to Jenny's arm. Jenny dodged but stopped anyway, and there we all were, standing in the middle of the intersection while the cars were stopped.

"Where's Charlie?" Agnes asked her.

"He broke his arm while he was playing with Peter; he tumbled out of Peter's hands. I took him to Emergency, and the hospital wouldn't give him back."

"Oh my, oh my," Agnes said.

The cars began to move, and the three of them with the white dog went in one direction and we in the other, out of the path of the approaching traffic.

I looked back. They were continuing happily on their way, hesitating sometime like they weren't too sure where they wanted to go, but enjoying every moment. With them the white dog patiently was doing a virtual dance to stay abreast of her friend Peter as he lurched and wove. It was the first time I saw her standing clearly in full daylight. Her soiled white jacket rode high enough on her back that it showed how thin her body was, her ribs visible through her short, dirty fur atop her tall, spindly legs. She was not having a good life—although probably not much worse off than mine. We tramps don't have it easy. We have to accept what we can get. But there was one difference. I could always hope I'd get back to a comfortable life with Ted. The white dog had nothing to hope for; her lot was with Peter, and you could see it in her tired eyes. Children and dogs don't get a choice. Some are lucky, some aren't.

All the way home to our alley Agnes kept saying to herself, "Oh, my, oh, my." She was not her carefree self that day. Jenny had really messed us up.

13. MATHILDE

It was not long later that we wandered north up along Hudson River Park, far enough that I figured we were on our way to visit Mathilde. We found her sitting on a bench by the river. She was leaning forward, weeping, with her face in her hands. Without saying a word Agnes sat down beside her, and Mathilde looked up. "Oh, you have brought Fee-Fee," she exclaimed, with a smile through her tears. Agnes lifted me up onto the bench between them. Then there was silence. Agnes didn't ask what was wrong; she just waited.

Mathilde said, "I am glad you have come, Ang-yes. I am so glad to see you. How did you know I was lonely today?"

Agnes still didn't say anything, but she looked compassionately into the eyes of her friend. She took Mathilde's hand and held it with both her hands. Mathilde stroked my head with her free hand. "So cute, Fee-Fee," she said, and she broke again into a smile, a very quick one.

Mathilde hesitated tearfully. As if it was very hard for her to talk about, still crying some, she said, "I miss Versailles, the people, the court, the grand parties. Jean-Luc was such a handsome count there; I was his beautiful courtesan. When we escaped during the Revolution, what a terrible night! The horses drawing our carriage were running as fast as they could." She put her hand to her forehead. "What a memory! I am back there every night in my dreams." Then she said in a low voice like telling us a secret, "But here in New York, Jean-Luc forgets me. I wait and I wait." She raised her arm in a grand gesture, "And I need to buy groceries." Agnes kept a peaceful smile.

Mathilde continued less emotionally, more resignedly, "He is old, and he forgets." She waited. Agnes squeezed her hand. Mathilde smiled through her tears, "But when he comes to me, he says he still loves me very much." She said it hopefully, looking for agreement.

Agnes' eyes answered "Yes."

Mathilde stroked my head, "Fee-Fee, so pretty, like my Fee-Fee in Paris." Then, gazing out across the river, she added in a tired, sorrowful, faraway voice, "Probably out of loyalty, but not because he finds me interesting any more." Then she stood up and asked Agnes, "Do you want to go home?"

Agnes said, "Yes," and that's where we went. On the way she told Mathilde about Jenny and Charlie.

"Who's Charlie?" Mathilde asked, and got very quiet when she found out.

I never saw Jean-Luc, but I did meet Mathilde's son Jean-Pierre, which was not very pleasant at all. It was during that last trip there. I barked when I heard his key in the door. He let himself in without knocking. As soon as he saw Agnes, he yelled at his mother, "What are you doing with this vagabond?" When he spotted me, "And a vermin dog!" He said we were dirty and disgusting. *"C'est de la cochonnerie! C'est de la saloperie! De la saleté!"* He grabbed Agnes by the shoulder of her coat to drag her to the door. I growled and barked, and dodged when he kicked. Mathilde was on him in a flash, and she pushed him off Agnes hard.

"Stop it! *Arrête!"* she said very loud, and then she hissed, *"Silence!"* at him, her eyes piercing his like a snake's. Clearly she wasn't afraid of her son.

Jean-Pierre stood there, preppy in sports jacket and jeans, very pale, his neck-length black hair disheveled. He gazed back at his mother defiantly for a moment. I could see that he loathed her. He was shorter than Mathilde; his face, a younger male version of hers, twitched, then settled. "I need a loan," he said to her. "And I won't be back for a while; I promise."

"I am always very glad to see you, Jean-Pierre," Mathilde said to him gently. "But now is not a good time for you, *évidemment.* I can't make a loan right now. Maybe tomorrow. I am waiting for Jean-Luc. Come back tomorrow."

He turned to leave. "Ok, tomorrow, *à demain.*"

"In the meantime," Mathilde added, stopping him, "find your niece Jenny. She has a baby."

"What do I care!" Jean-Pierre objected.

"I care," Mathilde said to him firmly.

The man turned on his heels, and walked to the door. With his hand on the knob, he started to say something, changed his mind, and went out. I braced myself for the bang, but he didn't slam it.

Mathilde walked over to Agnes who was shaking.

She put her arm around her and said, "Don't worry, Angyes, there is no reason to be afraid. We will have supper and then we will go to the opera."

Supper was frozen dinners, served hot. I had to wait for mine to cool. Mathilde and Agnes napped in their chairs afterwards. Then we went out.

Evenings Mathilde and Agnes wandered about together, with me in tow. Invariably, no matter where else we went, we'd walk through Lincoln Center. This particular time was no different.

The two women's faces glowed happily as we ascended the wide steps, like little children's on entering a playground. We crossed into the large square, the huge glass-faced buildings rising up in lights on three sides. Mathilde and Agnes breathed deeply the grandeur as we circled slowly through the gathering crowd. People were entering one building or the other, not hesitating long outside, because the evening was cold. We didn't hurry; we walked the periphery twice, and then Agnes and Mathilde sat on the wide circular edge of the central fountain as people do. Agnes picked me up and held me under her coat because I was shivering. The two women held hands and gazed straight ahead at the Metropolitan Opera building, like it was the most wonderful thing they ever saw.

"It is by far the most impressive theater here," Mathilde remarked. "Look at how its lights glimmer, from floor to ceiling, and the ceiling is so high!"

"It's very pretty!" Agnes agreed.

"Oh, I love *la richesse*. I love the parties. I love the

theater. I so love the opera. I love being rich," Mathilde said. "I can't get enough of it. I just can't get enough. Look, Agnes, how splendid it is."

The two women continued to sit there with the fascination of children, sometimes silent, watching the world of theater-goers swirl around them. Agnes didn't say much. Then she stretched out her legs and leaned back, so I was afraid she'd fall into the fountain. I was ready to jump off her lap at any moment. She clapped her stubby hands, and people passing by turned their heads away from the attention she didn't mean to bring to herself. "Oh, Mathilde, the sky is full of stars," she said. "Look, like the Opera lights."

After a while, Mathilde stood up. "Well, I don't know where Jean-Luc is," she said impatiently. "I guess I'll just have to go in without him." She held out her hand to Agnes, "Good-bye, *chère* Ang-yes, I hope you will come back soon." And she strode forward, in her tattered, long lace dress with the fox fur, and her broad-brimmed ribboned hat, a solitary figure walking like a grande dame. People stepped out of her way. Some stared.

"Eccentric and bizarre," one said.

"With stories to tell," another answered.

Mathilde passed through the doors of the Metropolitan Opera, and beyond the glass we could see her in the immense lobby. There she moved from one position to another, sometimes to the wall to look at a display, then by the doors as if she were waiting for someone. Mostly she kept crossing slowly, politely excusing herself, through the crowd that was filing its way past the ticket-takers, like a fish swimming in and out of other fish swimming by. She never approached the ticket-takers, however.

I could always see Agnes' joy at Lincoln Center. She loved the lights. She loved the people, and she could enjoy being among them without joining in as Mathilde needed to do. She sighed, and she sighed again. "You know, though, Precious, I think I love the stars best of all tonight," she said to me. Then, "It's cold; let's walk." She'd been holding me under her coat since I'd started shivering. She put me down now, and I could stay reasonably warm so long as we kept moving. We walked the periphery of Lincoln Center Square again, with Agnes sighing from time to time; and then we walked right out of it.

That night we made it to the shed. However, someone else had found it, too. When Agnes opened the door, the surprised person awoke and gave a loud grunt. Agnes closed the door, and we kept going. After more long, weary walking, we made it to our alleyway. Agnes collapsed on our bed of blankets and coats. She pulled them over her; then she thought of me and removed my twine leash. My harness was too much for her so she never tried. I hadn't had it off me since Ted. I crawled under the blankets with her, and we fell asleep.

Agnes might have heard Mack coming, and she might've been a little faster, if she hadn't been so tired. I heard him. I would have a mile away. I heard his footsteps, and when I looked out from under the blanket, the shadow I saw terrified me. Staggering, feeling his way along the alley wall, he was so out of his mind he could hardly walk. My barking confused him for a moment, and Agnes certainly startled him when she finally jumped up; but it just put him into a rage. She was in the middle of the stuff he wanted to tear open; she was in his way. When he pummeled her and flung her off him, it was dark, and he was crazed. She probably would've called out his name if she'd had time to know who it was; and if she'd done so, he might've known who she was and not have hurt her so badly. Or maybe he was just too crazy.

I ran and ran, hid freezing under the tarp by the construction site, and when I could stand the cold no longer, returned then to Agnes' blankets in our alley. Eventually I had to go out to find food. That's when I made my way down Seventh Avenue to the Village, and decided to retrace the route home that Ted and I used to take after going to the bank.

14. MOLLY

Reaching Waverly Place, I paused at the corner by Three Lives Bookstore, then crossed the street to sniff the spot near Julius' Bar where I'd lost Ted. Now I'd lost my friend Agnes, too. It seemed I kept losing everyone I cared about.

Ted was back, though; I was sure I'd seen him. So I kept going the way home. I walked to our building, hesitated at the steps, then ran up the left side just the way I always insisted on doing it. The front door was closed, so I lay down to wait for someone to open it for me. It took a long time, and I was shivering with cold when a man finally came out. I looked up to see who it was. That gave him time to block my entry with his foot. When I snapped at his ankle, he pushed me off the landing with a kick. He stood at the top looking down at me, and I stood at the bottom looking up at him. I barked for him to let me in; it was so frustrating. All I had to do was to get inside and wait by our apartment door until Ted came out. The man came down the steps towards me, and I ran. I was too cold to wait about any longer; I had to get moving. I ran back to the only place I had.

Agnes' blankets were still in the alley. I could be warm under them until I managed to get home. I hid there during the day and foraged at night.

I made the circuit of grocery stores as I used to do

with Agnes, but all their garbage was sealed. Agnes was able to open the bags, but I didn't know how. So I had to be content with the spillover of the street corner trash cans. It required a lot more traveling to find anything, down the avenues from trash can to trash can. I'd trot along to cover distance, and trotting kept me warmer, too.

One night, at the darkest quietest hour, the safest time when the fewest people were out about, somewhere on the Far West Side, I came around a corner onto Tenth Avenue and found myself suddenly face to face with Molly. The pit bull was out on her own. I was truly startled. The hair on my shoulders bristled, I growled, and we were so close I snapped at her. My back tense, my tail straight up, I was totally ready to run. Molly didn't rush me. On high alert I sniffed noses with her. When she made the slightest move, I jumped away. She waited, and we sniffed again. But I could sense only good from Molly; her signals were all positive, and I relaxed. I answered hers with my own then; I began to wag my tail—the best signal there is. Molly licked my face, and then we nose-kissed again, like two old friends meeting.

Molly continued on, but I preferred not remaining alone, so I followed behind her. Soon we were trotting along side by side. As Molly picked up the pace, I enjoyed the sense that we were two free spirits together. It was the first time I began not to feel bad about being lost.

Side-by-side, Molly was still in the lead. She brought me to the bags of garbage put out on the curb by restaurants up and down the Chelsea avenues. I watched her begin by sniffing their surfaces. When she smelled something she wanted, she did a quick digging action with her front paws on the bag. That made a hole in the plastic just big enough to expose the morsel. Using my nose I learned to get choosy, too. Most importantly, by imitating Molly's digging, I found that the claws on my much smaller feet were sharp enough to make a hole, as well.

It didn't take us long to satisfy our hunger. The slightest beginning of dawn began to turn darkness to grey, and we both knew to get back into hiding. Molly didn't invite me to follow her. She went her way, and I went mine, back to Agnes' blankets in the alley.

The next night when it was time to go out again, I wanted Molly's company; so I headed for the corner where I'd met her. It was a bit of a trek northward from my alley, but it was worth it, because there was Molly coming down the avenue. We met up, greeted each other with nose-kisses, and headed for the restaurants. It was another good night with good food: chicken, and steak trimmings, and cheese pastas, and cooked vegetables like Ted used to give me, sweet potatoes and carrots and broccoli. I even found some ice-cream containers I could clean-lick. I mean, this was the best I'd had since losing Ted. Molly didn't scatter things all over the place; she made a hole in a bag only as big as she needed, and so I did the same. She also didn't lead me to the same restaurants night after night. She always went to different ones, so no one would be waiting to catch her. Molly was a very wise dog; I was lucky to be her friend.

We'd been doing this quite a few nights, at the end of each of which Molly and I would part. She'd go her way, and I'd go mine. This was becoming our routine. I didn't think much about it. Then one morning when I got back to my alley at the crack of dawn, two men were there sweeping up all of Agnes' possessions and putting them in garbage bags, without folding anything the way she did. I stood off to the corner watching. They just crammed everything into the bags, and their sweepings on top of it, making a mess of Agnes' things. They stacked the bags at the curb and moved on with their big brooms. While I waited there wondering what to do, a big white garbage truck stopped by, and two other burly men tossed the bags into the back of it. One pulled a lever and a massive blade came down and scooped all of Agnes' stuff into the maw. And they drove off, stopping farther up the street for other waiting bags.

I checked out my alley. Standing stationary outside had gotten me shivering again. It was swept clean. There were no blankets, nothing, nothing left. While I hesitated, I grew colder; the winter chill went right through me. I needed to get warm. It meant I had to run, and it meant I had to find another hideaway where I could stay warm while I slept. There was only one place I knew of, as much as I'd always avoided the area for fear of running into Mack, and that was Agnes' shed beneath the buses' bridge. Heat rose from a grate in the ground. We'd always been warm there since the onset of winter, sometimes almost too warm.

What about the person who'd taken it over the last night we'd tried to go there, the fateful night of Mack's attack? I didn't even think about the person; I only thought about the heat. I was so chilled now from waiting while the alley was being cleaned out that I couldn't stay still. I ran, and ran, and I warmed up that way. Running, I soon reached the shed.

15. FAMILY

What a surprise I got! The person wasn't there anymore. Wonderful! But Molly was in the shed. The door was ajar, and she growled menacingly when I pushed my nose through the narrow opening. I stopped, and I whined to enter. She growled again, not fiercely enough to prevent me, but warning me to keep my distance. By now I understood why. I could hear, smell and, in the early morning light, see her five tiny pups. She must've already suckled them because they were asleep, hardly stirring, on the blankets Agnes had left there right over the heat vent. The shed was cozy. I lay on an edge of the blanket by the wall, facing them. With my chin resting on my forepaws, I watched them, until I fell asleep.

From then on I lived with Molly in the shed. Molly and I would go out foraging every night and then return before dawn. She'd suckle her pups whose eyes were open now. She taught them to be quiet when they'd start to squeal. She fed them; she licked them clean; she loved them as they cuddled in a pile of little bodies against her. One morning I nudged the pups a bit for a better place on the bed. Molly didn't mind. I joined the heap; we all kept each other snug.

I felt like Molly had chosen me. When a tattered old German Shepherd came near the shed one morning, Molly wouldn't let him in. She warned him off with a growl, and he went away. He may have been the pups' father, because three of them looked pit bull, but two had faces that were more German Shepherd. Those two and one of the little pit bulls also had black and tan coloring like a Shepherd, just like I surprisingly do, too. One pit bull pup was solid gray with white on her face like Molly; one was almost totally black.

So began my life with Molly and the pups. Each night when Molly and I would leave them to go out into the dark when the city was at its quietest, I could sense her worry. She'd nose the blanket over them, and they'd be silent. She'd no choice; she had to eat well, those quality restaurant foods we found, to produce a flow of milk to suckle them when we returned.

Molly usually didn't pay much attention to passing cars when we were out foraging. But one night she tensed, whined, and gave me a warning bark. She had some experience with the Animal Control van coming down the street that scared her. It was easy to spot, all white with black lettering and an orange light on its roof. It stopped, and a man got out. I didn't know what to think, but Molly signaled "Run!" and we did as fast as we could. He jumped back into the van and pursued us down the street. We escaped easily when he spotted the bedraggled German Shepherd standing on the corner and stopped for him instead. The old dog didn't run, but instead wagged his tail friendlily when the officer enticed him. The Shepherd only began to struggle when he was collared, and then it was too late. Molly led me on a very circuitous route to return to the pups. I learned to do that, too.

It felt so good after each night's foraging to get back to the warmth of the shed. Molly would organize herself on the blanket against the far wall, as her plump puppies jostled for position to drink their fill. Afterwards, with the heat from the ground source coming up through the blankets, we'd all nod off to sleep. The days went by lazily that way. Molly fed her pups faithfully at intervals, and they grew fast.

Time passed. It stopped being so cold when we stepped out of the shed at night. It began to feel good to get out. We also had less time to forage, because the first light of dawn appeared sooner each day. Even as the nights grew shorter, we tried to go out only in the deepest dark.

I could smell the change in the air, the fragrance of early flowers in the tree beds and in the parks. I felt drawn to happy times I'd had in daylight. I remembered walking along the river mornings with Agnes. I remembered running the beach on the Island with Ted, although that was becoming a more distant, diffuse thought. Life with Ted was fading, like my own puppyhood in Oklahoma. Despite my desire to go out, I trusted Molly. She was a wise dog, and she and her pups had become my cherished family now. I continued to let her lead. When I'd been alone and fearful, I'd figured out for myself to stay hidden until nighttime. That didn't stop my yearning.

The puppies were getting big. Still feeding them her milk in the shed, Molly began to bring them out with us on short trips to forage for solid food in the warmer air. This was a frightening time for Molly and me. She had to teach the pups to be aware, and that those trips were not play time. She had to teach them to recognize the van, and to keep away from people. One pup, the little Shepherd female, was too friendly and ended up being grabbed up by a person on the street. It's only when Molly threatened with a loud bark and crouched ready to spring, that the puppy was put back down. We ran fast, the troop of us. We just were getting too obvious.

It became increasingly difficult to make it back to the shed before dawn. Someone standing by would have no trouble seeing us enter it. It was on such a morning that returning up Tenth Avenue in the early light Molly and I suddenly froze in our steps. The puppies, of course, didn't know the difference. There in the middle of the street, with cars slamming on their brakes to avoid him, was Mack, in a filthy yellow T-shirt, brown shorts and a grimy khaki jacket, doing a drugged dance. He was reaching up towards the sky, then stooping to a crouch, then whirling in slow motion like a ninja with his arms out, then prancing with knees high. Molly hesitated, thinking fast which way to flee, because it seemed he would head toward us. Then he turned and walked away through the traffic as if the cars weren't whizzing by him, and made it to the other side. He took off his coat, wrapped it around a lamppost and buttoned it up like he was putting it on somebody. Then he turned and yelled, "It's legal to kill bald eagles, so long as you use all the feathers. You can kill them. You can kill them. You just have to use all the feathers." He was oblivious to everything around him.

Molly led us at a run up the street, and across another block to our shed. It was as if she couldn't get us through the door fast enough. She was nervous, and didn't fall asleep after the pups suckled, but stayed alert. She napped only fitfully during the day. I slept alright, and it's a good thing I did. The warm shed had outlived its usefulness. It was too difficult now to keep the pups hidden, and they needed to be able to run about. Sighting Mack gave her the final push. She knew she had to move them.

16. THE NORTH WOODS

As soon as it got dark, Molly and I went out. She had suckled the puppies again a while before, and now made them wait in the shed while she and I found some food by the closest restaurants. She didn't give us time to eat a lot, only what we needed, and we returned to the shed. She didn't go in, but called the pups with a low throaty sound. They tumbled out, quite glad to be outside. Molly led us the short distance across to Hudson River Park. She and I never went there, because it wasn't a food source. However, tonight she knew that for her long trek it'd be perfect, because it extended endlessly northward, uninterrupted by cross streets, and we'd encounter almost no one there after dark. She led the way. The puppies trotted along behind her. I followed last to make sure they kept up and didn't let their curiosity about this or that make them stray.

We traveled steadily, mostly at a trot. Even when Molly slowed to a walk, her longer strides kept us at a quick pace. She conveyed her urgency. If the puppies needed a rest, she led them into bushes and let them lie down until their panting stopped. Then we moved on northward. When we came to where Agnes and I used to meet Mathilde, I saw Mathilde sitting on a bench not far from a street light. We trotted on by. The park extended endlessly forward into the dark, and we continued a distance I'd never gone.

At 100th Street Molly turned and led us through an arch that crossed beneath the Westside Highway to the terraces of Riverside Park. She knew her way on the paths, and with her pups ran up the sets of steps to the street. I don't like stairs because I trip on them, so I hesitated; but I had no choice. I had to muster my courage or be left standing alone at the bottom. I caught up, and we hurried block after block down a sidewalk lined with buildings much like downtown. We still had the cover of darkness, and not many people were out.

Molly and I knew how to cross the avenues, carefully. Street-crossing was an important lesson the pups would have to learn, but right now they simply followed their mother. Past Broadway, and Amsterdam Avenue, and Columbus Avenue, we reached the northwestern corner of Central Park. Molly led us into it, all the way to an interior area called The North Woods. She'd chosen this wilder, more deserted landscape to finish raising her pups. The trees and bushes were growing leaves, and soon thick foliage would keep her family quite invisible; and if they had to run, they could escape in any direction without being blocked by buildings.

The earliest light of dawn showed us our way now. Molly led us down several curving paved paths, past a pond, past a waterfall, through a tunnel, then around low, craggy hills on dirt paths, then off the paths up a rise until she came to a stone outcropping. Beneath it, around a boulder, she brought us to a sheltered little cave, a few feet deep. She led us inside.

This was it. She couldn't have had her pups here in mid-winter; they'd have frozen. But now in warmer air, it was perfect. The stone outcropping, the depth of the cave, and the slope of the hill would keep rain out. Well-hidden among the trees and undergrowth, the den had play space in front of it for the pups. Below, the run-off from the pond created a small stream, so there was water close by, too.   Molly was so smart. What else could we possibly want?

Home life at the den became quite idyllic. There the months of approaching summer were among the happiest I've ever known. Leaves filled the trees and covered the bushes, and vines made the foliage dense, so we were well-hidden. The pups enjoyed a normal life. They could tumble out of the den in daylight and play and roll and wrestle in front of it and on the hillside, to their hearts' content. Molly and I would lie together in the den entrance, side by side, watching them. We all still slept a lot during the day—lots of naps—because our foraging trips for food continued at night, along the streets surrounding the park, as we had done downtown. We found a butcher shop's bags with wonderful meat trimmings we added to the menu. Occasionally Molly and the pups would carry a few bones back to the den, but Molly didn't make a habit of that. Nor did she let us raid the same places on a regular basis. One night we went in one direction; the next night we went in an opposite one. So we didn't get any of the restaurants too excited about the holes in their bags.

Molly was a good mother. She also was a good

teacher, which is an important part of being a good mother in our world. The first lesson she persevered in teaching the pups was how to cross the street safely. They tended to be impatient, impulsive, but she made them wait not only until the traffic passed, but taught them to look down the street to make sure more was not approaching. Only when there was a safe opportunity to cross did she give them the signal. Eventually, she let one or the other of them give the signal, and if it was wrong she countermanded it. If it was right, she confirmed it, and we crossed. I always thought I had crossing streets figured out, but I'd had some close calls because I didn't think enough about how fast cars were coming. I learned a lot from Molly as she taught her pups.

An easy lesson was finding food in the restaurant garbage bags waiting for pick-up. But Molly didn't let the pups rip them open helter-skelter as they were inclined to do. She taught them, as she'd taught me, to smell the surface of the bags, and then to claw a small hole only where the morsel was located. With Molly, we didn't scatter garbage all over the place, so we didn't get people mad about a mess. She understood we shouldn't advertise that we were around. The pups learned by her example.

Back at the den she conveyed the importance of quiet to the pups, so none of them became yappers. They'd roll and wrestle and chase, silently. No noise. Just the cracking of twigs and rustling of leaves, hardly distinguishable from the noise the squirrels made scampering around. Her warnings when they chased too close to the edge of the foliage cover were meant to teach them to be careful in this regard, to remain concealed. They didn't fear people; they'd been given no reason so far to be afraid—both Molly and I had known good people— but they learned to stay away from them, out of sight, because people don't understand dog freedom. For some reason, people can't tolerate it. I'd already learned that.

Living in captivity among people, with Ted even, was the price of being cared for, of being allowed. It meant being submissive, being told. I did not know anything different. Ted decided what to do, and in exchange I got a safe home and food—and his friendship, which I loved. However, I was enjoying food and a home now as a free dog. Now Molly was my friend. In a few months I'd gone back with her to a life that, deep down inside me, felt more natural.

The three little pit bulls were very active, and Molly had to keep a close eye on them. Soon they were twice bigger than me, too big for Molly to pick up any longer by the scruff of the neck when they got into trouble. They liked to rough-house, and sometimes they'd try it on me. I'd growl them a warning, but that wasn't always enough. I figured out how to handle them, though. I'd snap when they pushed their luck, and I found that a nip on the tip of the nose worked just fine. They'd give a pained yelp and go whimpering to Molly, and she'd give them a "Well, what did you expect?" look. No pity there.

The Shepherd male pup was a bit calmer, but quite willing to roll around with the three pit bulls, playing hide-and-seek and catch-me-if-you-can. The little Shepherd female, smaller than the other pups, gentler and friendlier, less wary, was devoted to her mother Molly, and seldom left her side.

17. ACCIDENTS HAPPEN

When we returned from foraging with our bellies full, the first thing we did at the den is nap it off. However, the pups didn't sleep long. Early morning Molly could let them run free, before people started coming into the park.

One such morning, when balmy spring was still in the air, we had our first accident. The pups were exploring the steep slope that leads to the Blockhouse, a small, square stone fortress not far from our den. We'd been there many times before. They were running all over the accessible side of the hill. When a couple of them reached the barred door, they began to nose around the structure. The fort is built at the edge of a cliff, with only a narrow path around the far side. It had rained, and the rocks were wet. The black pit bull pup lost his footing and slid over the edge. He tried to hold on with his forepaws, but his body hanging in space was too heavy. He tried and tried, but couldn't get back up, and he dropped. He fell on a stone edge at the bottom that broke his back.

I and the pups looked down from the ledge. The black pup below, bent like an elbow, was screaming. The top of his body was thrashing, and his front legs beating the air, but the back half of him wasn't moving at all. Molly ran down the slope to his side. When he saw his mother, he grew quieter. He whimpered, as if he expected her to fix things the way she always did. Then his eyes went far away. He stopped moving; he just lay there panting. There was nothing Molly could do, and she knew it. The pup, grown half her size, was her baby. She lay beside him and licked him, the length of his body, and licked, and licked. She kept licking him until his breathing stopped and he was still. She sniffed him a few times; then she looked up at us so sadly. She growled a throaty signal for us to return to the den. I made sure the pups got there, then I doubled back. Hidden at the edge of the thicket, I lay down too, and watched Molly who remained by her dead pup.

People came into the park. When a couple walked by, Molly remained quietly by the pup's body. One took out his phone, and in a while Animal Control came down the path. They picked up the pup and tossed him into their truck. Then they tried to catch Molly, but she ran off in the direction opposite the den, and easily got away. She didn't return to us until she knew they were gone. Unfortunately, they were alerted now to Molly's presence in the park, and the possibility she wasn't alone. They drove up the pathways almost daily after that, but made no effort to scour the woods. Molly kept us close to the den. We left only at night to forage. Molly was sad for many days, hardly communicating with me or the pups at all. I respected that.

After a while our life returned to normal. Animal Control's visits to our area tapered off; they probably figured that Molly had moved on. We foraged at night.

Molly continued teaching the pups. She and I lay contentedly side by side in the opening to the den watching them play outside. We didn't ever again go near the Blockhouse, except only Molly who went occasionally to sniff the spot where her pup had fallen. The days grew hot. Even the energetic pups preferred to nap in the shade daytimes when the sun was highest in the sky. Life was good.

However, I don't seem to be able to hold on to happy times very long. One of those hot days Molly rose to go down to the stream for a drink. I watched her descend the hill. Suddenly she jumped straight up into the air as if she'd been stung by a bee. She'd stepped on a fishhook, dropped by some careless child who'd been fishing the stream. She lay down right there at first and licked her forepaw where the hook was embedded. Finally she limped back up the hill to the den and continued, off and on, to lick her paw through most of the afternoon.

The fishhook was at first a sore annoyance, especially when it made it harder for her to forage at night. It got worse during the following days. Molly's foot swelled. She could hardly walk on it and began to sleep a lot. When she was awake, her eyes were glassy, and her few movements sluggish. I could tell she was in a lot of pain, but she suffered quietly as dogs do. The third night she didn't stir to go foraging, so I led three pups out alone. The little Shepherd female remained by her mother. The fourth night Molly had to eat, so she tried to go with us. I felt very worried to see her limping so badly, and whining to herself from time to time with pain. When we made it to the edge of the park, she had to stop. I and the pups crossed the street and waited for her on the other side. She finally crossed. She fed from some garbage bags close-by, hardly eating anything, and we returned to the park. She paused so many times, and for such a long time when she did, that it was getting light when she limped with her family, slowly, painfully, toward the path leading to our den.

That's when the Animal Control vehicle came around the curve. There was no putt-putt to warn us as in the past. This one was a new kind, and it moved silently. With all our focus on Molly, we were quite taken by surprise. Molly gave her throaty signal, and I and the pups scattered and escaped. Poor Molly, try as she did, could not run, either for her excruciating paw or for her swimming brain. One of the men snared her. The second man simply picked up the Shepherd female, always too-friendly, and loyal, who had hesitated by her mother's side. Molly struggled mightily then, as if she'd just awakened—she didn't want to be separated from her pups—but there was little she could do when the collar tightened around her neck. Subdued, she was heaved onto the truck, into a cage where the Shepherd female already awaited her mother. The presence of her little female pup with her calmed Molly somewhat, together with her pain, and from a distance I watched the truck pull silently away with Molly and her daughter riding placidly in the back.

I waited a long time before going back to the den, wandering around the area to make sure that Animal Control was gone. I found that the three remaining pups, the Shepherd-colored pit bull, the grey pit bull with white face who resembled Molly, and the Shepherd male, had all come back before I had. They still were so inexperienced. No prudence whatsoever!

18. THE POOL

In the weeks that followed, I did my best to take care of Molly's children. They gave me some respect when I tried to restrain them, but mostly they didn't pay much attention at all and did whatever they liked. I feared discovery. If Animal Control had returned looking for Molly, then they'd be back again, because now they'd seen all of us. The two pit bull pups were the adventurous ones, and it didn't take them long to get into trouble. Molly used to allow them some leeway early mornings, but now they started running around in the daytime. Pretty soon, with their new freedom, they became quite fearless.

Within our area, in the northwestern corner of Central Park, there is a beautiful woodland pond named The Pool. It lies close to the west wall below The Great Hill, feeding the stream that meanders beneath the rise in The North Woods where we lived. I began to enjoy leaving our foliage-enclosed den, as safe as it was and cool at midday, for a space where I could sun and view a wider landscape. Near the base of The Great Hill there are stone outcroppings overlooking The Pool that afforded me that luxury. Their flat surfaces were high enough to survey all of the pond's little valley, hidden enough above the paths, and cool enough when I desired the shade of a thicket close by.

I was there one afternoon in and out of dosing when

I was yanked awake by the panicked quacking and honking and splashing of the birds that frequented the pond's shoreline. What was usually a tranquil place exploded. The geese making an angry racket were rushing to the center of the pond, while the ducks fleeing into the water from land's edge took flight together in a woodland swoosh. The two pit bull pups, almost full-grown now, were up to their bellies in the water, panting, and looking quite satisfied with themselves. All of the people on the paths who saw it happen were horrified. The two pups trotted off together and disappeared into the under-growth in the direction of our den.

The young pit bulls liked very much this new sport they'd discovered, chasing the ducks and geese at the pond. It wasn't long before they added one more game, stalking the food people tossed to the birds. They'd hide, and when the morsel landed on the ground, they'd jump out and grab it, scattering the birds again and frightening the people. They were having such a good time that there was no way I could stop them. Seeing them heading for the pond, I'd imitate the throaty bark and growl Molly did, but I couldn't convince them. They paid me no attention. They were getting older, and they were having a good time.

People had no problem disobeying the posted signs not to feed the wildlife, but everyone was really annoyed that somebody was ignoring the ones that forbade letting dogs run about off-leash. As the birds scattered, one person would say, "The signs say dogs aren't allowed in the water," and another would say, "Where's the owner?"

They'd look around to figure out who the owner was. Then they'd take out their phones, and that brought Animal Control.

I knew the pups were going to wreck things not just for themselves, but for me, too. I could feel it coming. At first, instead of going off by myself as I'd begun to do, I stayed with them. I tried to entice them away from the pond. Only one of them stuck closer by me, the Shepherd male, even though he sometimes got pulled into the fun. He became more and more my friend.

When I wasn't able to stop the pups' rampages through the park, my fear of the disaster they were attracting led me to change my strategy. Instead, I left them alone daytimes, got as far away from the trouble as I could. I returned to my perch on the side of The Great Hill as I loved to do these beautiful summer days. I even had a place under an outcrop where I could lie on a rainy day—the little valley was pretty in the rain, too. Usually the Shepherd male accompanied me. More sensitive to the heat than I was, because of his longer hair, he lay in the shade beneath the thicket looking out. He seemed as enchanted by the place as I, and soon fell asleep.

Late morning one day not long after the pups' disturbances began, my fear was realized. I'd just reached my ledge beneath The Great Hill, and the Shepherd male was concealed in the thicket, when I saw across the pond two Animal Control officers arrive on foot and descend the low southern slope where the pups usually appeared. The men separated to take up positions on each side of the wood-chip peninsula the birds favored. The first officer occupied a nearby bench as anyone walking the path might do; the other waited quietly among trees which the pups themselves sometimes used for ambush. If only the pups would play the ambush game today, they'd spot the officer there.

That morning the two pups showed up instead running over the southern hill, straight for the birds on the peninsula. Loving the ruckus, they chased the quacking, splashing ducks right into the pond. The two officers came from behind. Because the pups had grown used to having people around, they were not alarmed. Only when they turned back in the water, they realized the two men were coming at them. They tried to escape, but they couldn't run in water as fast as they could on land. As he leapt past one of the officers and drenched him, the Shepherd-colored pit bull was snagged. He pulled and jumped and struggled and yelped, but the officer held him tight. The other officer didn't ply his collar so well, and the Molly-like pit bull got away. She headed straight for the woods and was gone.

I watched it all from the hill, and I didn't move. No one ever noticed me there, and the Shepherd male was out of sight beneath the bush. The Animal Control officers disappeared up the path over the rise from where they'd come, one of them leading the still struggling pit bull pup.

When I returned to the den sometime later, the Molly-like pup was lying as far as she could get against the back wall. I went to her and licked her to comfort her. She kept away from the pond after that. She held closer to the den, quiet and sad, mourning the loss of her companion, her brother, the Shepherd-colored pit bull pup.

The Molly-like pup was the most beautiful of the litter. She'd grown bigger than any of her mates. She had a wonderfully supple grey muscular body, and a huge, oversized white head like her mother's. Her wide mouth seemed in a perpetual smile. However, the mischievous look that had so characterized her eyes was gone now. She had entered a sadness that did not lift.

There were toadstools growing here and there on the ground in the woodland where we had our den. None of us ever thought they might be food, but the Molly-like pup started eating them one day. With her hind quarters dragging paralyzed behind her, she tried to pull herself home to the den. But she never made it. Still some distance away, she died during the night by the path. I kept vigil until morning with the Shepherd male. Then a park vehicle came by, and she was tossed into a garbage barrel it was carrying.

I went home to the den with the remaining pup, very sad. How'd everything that'd been so perfect gone so wrong now? I was growing weary. Since losing Ted my life was just one mess after another. I felt very alone. But I wasn't. The Shepherd male lay down beside me; he pressed his nose against my side, and whined softly. He was five times my size now, but he was counting on me. For Molly's sake, I wouldn't let him down. And with him, I still wasn't alone.

19. POOR BOY

I stopped being sad, and I passed the days that summer with the Shepherd male. He was attentive, faithful, thoughtful even. I liked him a lot. He chose to depend on me. I was leader of the pack, but we were friends.

One good thing about being only two dogs, and calmer ones, we didn't have to worry about being noticed so easily. I was small, and the Shepherd male was careful. We moved about sometimes during daylight, but most days sunned quietly on the side of The Great Hill.

It was one such beautiful day that looking down across the pond I thought I recognized Poor Boy sitting on the bench constructed of small logs that was in the middle of the wood-chip peninsula. He had a large white pad on his lap and was sketching the ducks and geese that were standing close by him at water's edge. I remembered his approaching with his blind mother on the street when Mack had a For Sale sign hanging around my neck. He had grown in a year, was longer and lankier now. He looked up and his eyes scanned my shore, and I wondered if he saw me. For a while I watched him across the water. Then as the sun was getting lower, he got up and left. I met the Shepherd male who was waiting for me under the bush, and we went back to the den.

I returned to the pond on a daily basis, attracted as

much now by Poor Boy who appeared regularly with his sketch pad. He did see me, and we looked at each other across the water. A few times I met him on the paths. Each time he stopped and spoke to me, staying far enough away. He didn't rush me. In my own time, at my own choosing, I approached closer to where he sat by the edge of the pond. Close enough to talk, he encouraged me. I could hear the calmness in his voice. I sensed his kindness. It was a warmth I'd known from Ted, but in Poor Boy stronger still. Ted always was busy with many things during the day. Poor Boy came to the park quietly and unhurried, connecting. Feelings from him touched everything, the birds, the squirrels, and me, especially me. I could feel him; it simply was in him. He loved everything alive, and that is the sentiment he conveyed. It didn't take long before I knew we could be friends, very special friends. Poor Boy began calling me Little Hobo.

But I wasn't alone. So I showed up one day with the Shepherd male. Poor Boy smiled surprised. Over the following weeks, the three of us became friends, slowly, carefully, the more so because the Shepherd male had no experience with people. But after his first wariness, he took to Poor Boy pretty naturally, too. Poor Boy named him Sunshine. I did not lead Poor Boy back to the den, though. That I reserved.

One day when he came to the pond, Poor Boy carried a leash. He wanted to attach it to my ragged harness. That was too much at first; I was a free dog now, and I didn't want to be restrained. Poor Boy, on the other hand, was thinking to "rescue" me and the Shepherd male, and he couldn't do it without the leash. Well, he certainly had slow going. It took half the rest of summer. I'd return to the den completely confused by it, drawn between my growing affection for Poor Boy, my loyalty to the Shepherd male, and the freedom I enjoyed in my woods.

Then evenings got cool, and nights got colder. Soon the leaves started to drop, buffeted by the winds, and it was not long before the den showed right through the trees. Staying in the park began to be not so great. So Poor Boy's warmth, both his tenderness and a warm home that I imagined he had, swayed me. I'd not entirely forgotten how cozy life had been with Ted. Sunshine was pretty calm about it all.

One day I let Poor Boy hook the leash to my harness. He did it almost without my noticing it, then he removed it. He did that often enough. He also persuaded Sunshine to accept a harness; Sunshine, becoming a very docile dog, allowed it following my example. Then we began walking on leash with Poor Boy in the park, quite proud of ourselves. Afterwards, he'd always release us.

Late one afternoon when the park didn't have many colored leaves left, and Poor Boy had just let us go, Animal Control came by. One of the officers came over and scolded him, threatening to confiscate us. "This isn't the first time we've seen these dogs off-leash. You know better than that. If they're off-leash again, we'll take 'em!" He asked Poor Boy to see our licenses. There weren't any, so the officer pointed his finger into Poor Boy's face and said, "And if you don't carry their licenses, we'll take 'em!" Poor Boy attached our leashes, and because of the danger we were in, while the officer watched, he left the park with us.

He led us down the avenue outside the wall, then took a right turn onto another street, and a block farther, a left turn. We were still west of the park. I trotted along, and Sunshine didn't mind, either. I knew it was time now for whatever was next. The nights were getting cold, and there wasn't any heat coming up from the ground into the den. Sunshine and I could share body warmth, but that still wasn't enough to keep me from shivering by morning. And now Animal Control was closing in; they knew about us and were watching to catch us. Yes, it was time to leave with Poor Boy.

20. DOCTOR FARLAND

We came to a heavy glass door with the words ANIMAL HOSPITAL written in big block letters upon it. Poor Boy knew he couldn't bring a feral dog like Sunshine into his home with his mother. Back then he probably had some doubts about me, too. Sunshine had never been inside a building before, and he reacted accordingly. Even though I trotted right through the doorway, he braced his feet and didn't want to cross the threshold. Poor Boy pulled on the leash gently, encouraging him in an even gentler voice, but Sunshine wouldn't budge. So I had to do something. I was already standing inside. I looked out at Sunshine and barked for him to follow. He looked at me, hesitated, then trotted through the door and sat on his haunches there in the lobby, looking at me as if to say, "Well, what's next?"

Poor Boy led us past the reception desk, saying to a woman behind it, "Please tell Doctor Farland I'm here with the wild dogs."

"Wild?" the woman exclaimed.

Poor Boy knew where he was going, and he led us forward to a large open room with many windows. It was like the one at dogs' daycare where Ted used to bring me to "socialize"—unsuccessfully. We entered the room through one door, and a man in a white coat appeared through another. His arrival made Sunshine nervous, but the man kept his distance.

"Well, they should be ok here," he said to Poor Boy. "Keep fresh water for them all the time. Feed them morning and evening. When you're not here, one of your fellow aides can check on them. But for a while you're going to have to be the one to walk them. Put down a training pad; see if the Chihuahua knows to use it. If he does, that should make the Shepherd begin to use it, too. And that's a goal, to get the dog accustomed to being indoors, calmer around people, and housebroken. That's a big order for a feral dog."

"I'll do it, Doctor Farland. I can. Thank you."

"I'm quite sure you can, John. You have a special way with animals. That's why I value your work here so much, and why I'm ready to help you with these two. Animals trust you. I've never met anyone who communicates with them as well as you can."

That's how I learned Poor Boy's name is John, and that he was working for Doctor Farland. The doctor communicated just fine, too; I liked him right away. But that didn't stop me from trying to snap at him when he put me on his examining table to check me over. It's simply what I do in that situation, how I behaved when Ted took me to the vet. I don't like the poking and prodding. Poor Boy held me tightly just like Ted did, and I got a little muzzle for the duration of the exam as always happened.

Doctor Farland didn't try to check Sunshine that way. "It's too soon," he told Poor Boy. "We have to give him time to develop more confidence."

That's how we lived for a while. Sunshine soon stopped trembling and got into the routine. Learning to be housebroken also came quickly to him because the training pad built on his instincts, just as it had for me when I was a pup.

I knew all about training pads. Ted didn't use them just for training; they were a permanent thing in our apartment. He always had one for me, replacing it with a fresh one whenever I used it. He'd encourage other dog owners when he saw them trying to train young puppies on the street, "We humans don't wait when we want to use the bathroom. Why should we put dogs through that? Would you like being limited to going to the bathroom twice a day?" He took me outside because I preferred doing my business on the street; and I'd wait to go out, so long as he was on time, but that was my choice. Sunshine did what Doctor Farland had hoped. He was curious where I went on the pad, and followed my example. We were walked three times a day, usually by Poor Boy wearing his veterinary-assistant's smock.

Both Sunshine and I liked the idea of having food provided for us twice a day. No more need for foraging. Sunshine got used to that really fast. He got used to having so many people around, too. After a while different persons would take us on our walks.

One day I found out why we weren't seeing Poor Boy so much. He came into our room with Doctor Farland, who was thinking deeply.

"I don't like to cut my hours," Poor Boy was explaining to the doctor, "I'd spend every minute here with the dogs and cats. But I get home from school, and my mother hasn't been out all day. She needs me to do errands and take her for walks."

"I understand, John, you certainly have to give her time. How's she doing, on her own?" the doctor asked.

"I enjoy taking her on walks. I'm her eyes. I tell her all the things I see. But we've got to live, and that's the errands. Getting stuff and things, I have to do it all. She's afraid to go out alone during the day with her cane."

"Afraid?"

"That someone will hurt her, to get her purse."

It was a few days later that I heard the rest of the conversation. Doctor Farland returned to it when he and Poor Boy were in the room with us. The doctor was sitting on the floor by Sunshine, patting him, and Sunshine was loving it.

"See what a fine dog Sunshine is," Doctor Farland said to Poor Boy. "He's beautiful. He looks like a German Shepherd and has that personality. But look at his haunches; they don't collapse like a Shepherd's. They're strong and stable, like a pit bull's. Sunshine has pit bull in him somewhere."

Poor Boy listened. I could feel the trust between them.

"Does your mother like dogs?" the doctor asked.

"I don't know. Before I started working here, we couldn't afford to have one."

"Bring her here, John. Let her meet Sunshine. If she likes him, you could take him home with you instead of finding a new owner like we planned. With Sunshine your mother could go out during the day if she wants to, while you're at school or working here. No one would think of bothering her if she has a dog that looks like Sunshine."

Poor Boy looked up at the doctor. He smiled. "What a wonderful idea! I'll have Little Hobo, and Mother would have Sunshine. Oh, that'd be wonderful. The two of us with our dogs."

21. MOTHER

That's what happened. Mother came to meet Sunshine. When he was brought out to her, Sunshine was very accepting; that's just how he was. He put his head on Mother's lap when she began to stroke him. Mother was unsure at first, but Sunshine was not; he sensed Mother's need. It was as if he knew the plan, and was ready to be a devoted dog. They communicated quietly, the blind woman and the gentle dog—the big, gentle dog.

Mother warmed to the idea more and more with each scheduled visit. She was a good woman, very kind, and mild. I'd heard Poor Boy explain to Doctor Farland that she was thrown off-balance by her handicap because it was new. She wasn't used to being blind; it made her feel vulnerable and afraid; she was still learning her way. She'd been a sighted person; only a few years ago, she'd been able to see. It was from her that Poor Boy got his kind disposition; it came from her. It overflowed in his love for animals. That's why he could talk to us. And Mother began talking to Sunshine.

Life was good at Doctor Farland's veterinary hospital. Both Sunshine and I didn't take long to become quite comfortable there. We lived in an area where Doctor Farland boarded dogs when their owners were away. These occasional residents supposedly contributed to our training which was entrusted to an assistant named Cathy. Sunshine was a natural; he got along fine. He had confidence, no matter how big the other dog was—and not many were bigger than Sunshine. He was gentle with the little ones; he was shoulder-to-shoulder with those his own size. He never was unfriendly, but he stood his ground if one of them over-asserted.

"What a beautiful dog," Doctor Farland would say when he looked at Sunshine. "So handsome, so noble."

Cathy might as well not have bothered trying to socialize me. I was used to dealing with other dogs my way. I like meeting little ones, especially Chihuahuas, most of the time—we Chihuahuas recognize each other. Any bigger dog, I let him know he'd better show respect. Ted used to say, "Someday you're going to start something you can't finish." I knew I could get away with attitude when I was walking with him, because all the dogs were on leash like me. I'd let them know it was my building and my street. Growl and snarl and jump against the end of the leash, it was great fun. I could expect Ted to exclaim, "Behave, behave!" and pull me back. Then I'd strut down the street, head high and tail straight up, so proud of myself. Ted would laugh and be amused and warn me, "You're so tough, Sweetheart, you think you're so tough. Someday one of these women out here with a big dog isn't going to be paying attention, or isn't going to be strong enough to hold on, and her dog will get away—and then you're going to be in big trouble with your leash game, Sweetheart."

Cathy was a professional trainer. Doctor Farland

asked her to put Sunshine through "finishing school" where he learned to follow lots of commands that Ted had never bothered me with, and Sunshine seemed to enjoy it. It wasn't too long before we were ready to go home with Poor Boy, both of us.

The apartment was very small. Perhaps Poor Boy thought he had to encourage me. "Mother's handicap got us city housing," he said to me when we got there. "We're really lucky to have it. And we're not far from Central Park, so we can take walks there." It had one bedroom, Mother's room, where Poor Boy set a bed for Sunshine at the foot of Mother's bed. Poor Boy slept on a cot in an alcove off the kitchen, and he put a bed for me under it. "How's that for cozy!" he said. I used it sometimes in the daytime; but it was not long before I was sleeping with him on his bed nights.

The idea was that with Sunshine along, Mother could go out on her own and not be afraid. She tried it a couple of times, holding Sunshine's leash with one hand, and with the other feeling her way with her white cane. It didn't work very well. She said, "It's too awkward, both hands busy like that." So she ended up not doing it much and continued to count on Poor Boy. Days while he was away at school it was pretty boring in that little apartment. Lying under the cot sure didn't compare to my perch at The Pool. I looked forward all day to the walks the four of us took together into the park.

22. SUNSHINE

One day when we were about to cross the street, Sunshine pulled back. I knew it was the training Molly had given him. He thought there was not enough distance from the oncoming cars. Poor Boy was surprised, but it gave him an idea. "Sunshine just acted like a guide dog, Mother. He held you back from the traffic. Wouldn't it be great if he could become a real guide dog? Wouldn't that make you feel surer?"

"It might," Mother answered. "I don't know."

Poor Boy had me with him the next day when he brought his idea to Doctor Farland.

"Well, it's not that simple," the doctor told him. "There are several guide-dog training schools in the vicinity of the city, but they breed their dogs themselves. They're specially bred for the job. Do you think your Mother would like one of them?"

"No," Poor Boy said.

That evening after dinner, when Mother was sitting in her chair quietly listening to her soft music that made Sunshine and me sleepy, and some time had passed that way, she asked Poor Boy, "What did Doctor Farland say?"

Poor Boy paused from his school work at the kitchen table. His enthusiasm for his big idea had been dampened. "He said the guide dog schools raise their own dogs. They breed them special." He hesitated. "He wants to know if you'd take one of those."

"No," Mother said resolutely. "No." Sunshine was resting his head on her lap as he so often did, and she stroked him gently. "Sunshine is special, *very special to me now*," and she reasoned, "What would happen to Sunshine if I got another dog? That dog would have to be my dog. What would happen to Sunshine? No."

Poor Boy paused. The doctor had cautioned him not to raise any false expectations. "Doctor Farland doesn't want you to get your hopes up for Sunshine. There's a possibility, but it's only a remote possibility." Then he told her the rest.

"Doctor Farland made a phone call to someone he knows at one of the schools. He told me afterwards that the school didn't want to take an outside dog, until he insisted how wonderful Sunshine is and that you wouldn't accept any other dog. I already told him what I figured your answer would be. Besides, I want to keep Sunshine, too. I told Doctor Farland, 'Better to leave it just as it is.'

"The lady at the school said that when Sunshine is eighteen months old, to bring him there. They'll give him the same test for intelligence and temperament and everything else as they use to decide which of their own dogs will be acceptable for training. Only if he can pass that test absolutely as well as their own dogs who get chosen, they'll do it—and still stop anytime they think it's a mistake."

"Well, that probably should be reassuring," Mother said. "If Sunshine learns to be a guide dog, that means he'll be just as good as any other." She was silent for a moment, then added, "For me, Sunshine will be better than any other. I know he loves me already, and I know how strong he is just from touching him. I'll never have to be afraid with him watching out for me."

"Mother," Poor Boy cautioned, "Doctor Farland says that as wonderful as Sunshine is, there's a good chance he won't pass the test."

"Then we'll just go on living as we are, won't we," Mother affirmed realistically.

Poor Boy told her the plan. "Doctor Farland will have Cathy train Sunshine very intensively over the next four months, so he'll be as ready as can be. That means that Sunshine is going to have to spend a lot of time with her. And you'll have to go to some of the sessions so Sunshine will understand that it's about you. Then if Sunshine passes the test, he'll have to be at the school for about six months. And the last month you'll have to be at the school with him. Is that all ok?"

Mother listened to her music a moment more before she answered, and she said with a little smile, "It looks like we're setting out on an adventure, all of us together. Things were getting a little dull around here, anyway. Sunshine will make it. We'll do it. And Sunshine, blessed Sunshine," as she stroked his head, "will be my freedom. Somehow I was waiting for something to happen, for a new phase to start, and this is it. I know Sunshine will succeed, and we'll succeed with him. I know he will."

And Sunshine did succeed. Months with Cathy, months at the school, a month with Mother at the school. And so Sunshine became a certified guide dog. Molly's pup. Molly I'd met in Mack's hovel, Molly who lived for her pups, Molly the good dog, the street dog, had a pup who became a guide dog, a special one, for Mother.

When we four went into the park now, Poor Boy had me on leash, and I trotted beside him. Mother held the handle to Sunshine's harness, and they walked together like one person. Poor Boy would tell Mother what he saw as he used to do, but now she'd tell him the birdsongs she heard or the scampering of a squirrel up a tree; she'd tell us how beautiful the air smelled with the fragrance of flowers. We'd sit together on a bench overlooking The Pool where I had so many memories. We were very happy together, the four of us.

When Poor Boy got home from school weekdays, he'd bring me to work with him at Doctor Farland's. I got to socialize with the boarders for a couple of hours whether I liked it or not. Some of the dogs were interesting, for a while anyway. When I got bored or just didn't want to bother with them, I'd fall asleep in a corner of the room. Then Poor Boy would come for me. We'd walk home together, and he'd tell me all about his day and his plans. Mother would have dinner ready for us. Afterwards, Poor Boy would do his homework with me sitting on his lap, and Mother would listen to her beautiful music with Sunshine resting by her.

23. KIDNAPPED

I have a hard time holding on to happiness. One day
on our way to work it all fell apart again. Someone came
from behind us on the street, grabbed my leash, and
yanked it out of Poor Boy's hand. It was Mack. "That's
my dog," he cried out. "You know that's my dog! What're
you doing with my dog! You stole him! You're a thief!"
And Mack was off with me.

Poor Boy was so surprised. He remembered how
he'd first seen me on the street with Mack, when I was
wearing the For Sale sign around my neck. Poor Boy
didn't know what to say. That's what Mack wanted, to
attack fast, to surprise, confuse him, and get away with me
before Poor Boy could even object. It was a mugging.
Poor Boy believed Mack, that I was Mack's dog. Helpless
and heart-broken, he watched us disappear down the
street.

Mack was walking so fast, pulling me so hard that I
had to run to keep up. If I'd been wearing a collar instead
of a harness, I'd have been choked he dragged me so
violently. When I started to scream he picked me up and
punched me, and carried me some distance so I wouldn't
slow him down. When I struggled to get free, he punched
me again, and again. People stared, and some objected,
but they got out of his way as he rushed past them. No
one was going to try to stop a wild man.

Mack brought me back to his apartment. It was all very familiar, but a worse dump than it had been, the home of a man crazier and crazier. And there was no Molly. Her presence there, her quiet, resigned company had helped me through those weeks before. This time I was alone with him. He put me down, and I ran to the farthest corner under the table. I couldn't hide, but I needed to get away from him as much as I could. Mack didn't care what I did. He was waiting for the person he'd called from a street phone when we were on our way in.

"Victor, this is Mack. I've got a dog for you.... Yeh, a Chihuahua.... A hundred... You're here in Manhattan? Right now?... Great. My place. As soon as you can; I've got to go out.... Ok, great. Great!"

I stayed trembling under the table, too frightened even to lick my hurts. Mack paced across the two rooms. Not *like* a madman; he *was* a madman. He rushed back and forth, back and forth. Sometimes he'd stop, and his body would twist like it did that day Molly and I saw him in the street. It seemed a long time went by, and then there was knock.

Mack opened the door to a thick-necked, pudgy man, who wheezed and wiped sweat from his forehead even though it was a cool spring day.

"Where's the dog?" Victor asked.

"Right there," Mack pointed to me.

Victor braced one hand on the table and leaned over to look under it at me. "Not much there. Fifty!"

"Fifty?" Mack exclaimed incredulously. "You said a hundred!"

"No, *you* said a hundred. I'm saying fifty."

Mack buried his face in his hands like he was going to cry. "Eighty?" he asked hopefully.

"Fifty," Victor said definitively.

"I could get a hundred for him on the street."

"Then do it."

Mack couldn't do it. He needed money now, right now!

Mack took the handful of crumpled bills, stuffed them into his pocket, and crawled under the table to pull me out. I didn't make it easy for him. I bit his hand hard when he reached for me. He jerked it back, but that didn't stop him and he came for me again. With a quick thrust of his bleeding hand, he grabbed me by the throat. I snarled, then screamed and fought as he dragged me out. He stood up holding me by the neck for Victor, my body swinging.

Victor held out a bag, and Mack dropped me into it. Then Victor tied the top like I was garbage. I thrashed and kicked inside it, and jumped and kicked all the way down the street to his car, where he tossed me into the back seat and drove off with me.

I soon had a hard time breathing. Without air, my senses whirled and I became totally panicked. I fought inside the bag, bouncing and rolling in it on the back seat until my kicking made a small hole. Then I lay there with my nose poked through, and that's how I rode the rest of the way.

Victor drove on and on for a long time before he finally stopped. When he reached in to pick up the bag with me in it, I began jumping and bumping again, and I opened another hole with my teeth. He carried me into a place where lots of dogs started barking, and he poured me out of the torn bag into a cage that was hardly big enough for me to turn around in, on top of another cage that had a dog in it. In all, there were six small cages like mine, stacked two on two, each holding one of the small breeds.

What alarmed me most were the very big dogs chained to wooden studs around the walls, spaced well apart, heavyweight pit bulls, with enormous heads like Molly had. All were badly scarred, mostly around their heads and necks, especially the old female. There were two males. The younger was less marked up, but the one in his prime at the end of the row had a face that had healed grotesquely. One side was normal, but the other side had been terribly torn, and hung down so that his eye had no bottom lid; his lip was ripped away and healed back into a big flap, so his teeth always showed. Whether he looked handsome or monstrous depended on which side faced you.

They all started a ruckus as soon as Victor walked in, barking to him and at me. Then I saw there was a pen built against the far wall. A mother pit bull was lying in it on a grimy bed with four almost full-grown pups. I thought of Molly when I saw her. Molly was old but beautiful. The face of this female was scarred, too. She looked very weary and didn't seem to care whether Victor came or went.

He left me there. I looked out from my cage in the dim light that came through the few small windows. I watched the dogs along the wall, tired, irritable dogs, desperate like Mack, but very quiet now instead. They lay there, stretched about, bored and resigned. And I looked down into the cramped cages below me, at terribly frightened dogs, like me. I trembled uncontrollably. I felt waves of cold pass through my body. This was worse than any nightmare I'd ever had. Every dog, big ones, little ones, was miserable. Except the pups; they went back to sleep alongside their mother.

In the cage under mine a Sheltie, small, timid, lay as extended as she could in the tiny space. She whimpered from time to time, then was silent. She was torn around her face and haunches. She seemed to be waiting—eyes wide open then closing—to fall away into sleep. And then she'd cry again. Some of her coat was soaked because I'd wetted in my fright, and it had dripped through the mesh of my cage onto her, and down to the dog under her.

24. ANGELA

A while later, as evening arrived and light grew dimmer, the door opened. A boy entered, about the same age as Poor Boy. He was followed by a little girl who had a very old female Chihuahua on leash.

"You know you're not supposed to be in here with me, Angela," the boy said.

"Oh, Freddy, I want to see the dogs."

"Then you stay near the door, and hold Tinker tight."

"Tinker Bell, stay right here with me," Angela reassured her Chihuahua.

Tinker Bell was smug, quite unconcerned by the mood of the other dogs. I watched her. She felt safe with Angela, but didn't like the shed.

Freddy began to feed all the dogs, pouring dry pellets into their dishes that lay at the ends of their chains. He replenished their water dishes as well. He spoke to each of them by name, to Princess and Buck and Thunder. By the time he'd finished feeding and watering us, too, in our stacked cages, the pit bulls had gulped down their food. Then Freddy walked Princess and Buck one at a time, using their chains for leashes to take them outside to the back yard. He let Manda go out free with her pups, and they jumped and played for a while before he called them back in. Only one dog didn't get a walk.

"Poppa will be home soon, Thunder; it won't be long. Be patient." Thunder was lying back by the wall, his good side facing out. He opened that one eye when Freddy spoke to him, then closed it again, like he didn't care.

Just then Angela, who'd watched Freddy doing his chores all this time, saw me. Pointing, she exclaimed, "Freddy, look, there's a Chihuahua."

"Yeh, prettier than Tinker," Freddy teased her.

"Tinker Bell is pretty, too," Angela insisted as she left her position by the door and walked over to me. My cage was high. She looked up, and I looked down.

"Freddy, I want to play with that Chihuahua. Please take him out for me."

"You don't want to make Poppa mad, do you?" he answered. "He'll be home any minute, and be coming in here. He has to take Thunder out."

As Angela left with Freddy, Tinker Bell in tow, she said, "I'm going to call him Topsy."

Soon Victor did come. He looked at Freddy's work, and then he took Thunder's chain and led the big dog into the yard. He made Thunder run on the chain in a circle around him. "That's it, Thunder. Run! Run! Run! Run! Devil, run! Run!" Victor called out as Thunder ran swiftly. "Run!"

Victor brought Thunder back inside, chained him up, turned off the light going out the door, and left us all in the dark. Soon there was just heavy breathing, some snoring, and sometimes whimpering. It was a very long night.

I awoke when first light began to appear through the small, high windows. I closed my eyes to fall back asleep as I normally would have done, but I was too anxious to sleep anymore. So I just watched the other dogs as they began to stir. The ones along the wall became alert together, almost at the same time; they knew their feeding schedule. Pretty soon Freddy opened the door, again with Angela and Tinker Bell close behind him. With them was their brother, younger than Freddy, older than Angela who was holding him by the hand. The boy didn't look very brave.

"Look, Mattie, see him up there," she said pointing to me. "That's Topsy. Isn't he pretty? I'm going to ask Poppa to give him to me, so he can play with Tinker Bell."

Beginning his chores, Freddy said, "Fat chance."

"Why not?" Angela protested.

"Because he gets annoyed enough with Tinker Bell. He gave you one dog. He's not going to give you another one," Freddy said to her knowingly, like he was putting an end to the matter.

Angela came over to my cage and looked up at me, while Mattie remained by the door where she'd attached Tinker Bell's leash. "Good morning, Topsy," she said to me. I cocked my head, trying to look my cutest. I sensed the goodness in Angela that pierced through the misery in the shed.

"I'm going," Mattie said. "I don't like it in here."

"But isn't he pretty?" Angela insisted.

Mattie was out the door. Freddy went about his chores, feeding and watering. He started exercising Princess and Buck and Manda and her pups. Unlike

Mattie, Angela wasn't afraid at all around the dogs in the shed. She remained quietly watching Freddy and looking at me. She waited patiently, and when Freddy was almost finished, she asked him, "Freddy, please take out Topsy. Look he already has his leash on." No one had yet removed the harness and leash I'd been wearing when Mack took me from Poor Boy.

Freddy gave Angela all the reasons why he shouldn't. She said then she'd just have to stay in the shed with me all day. Freddy gave in to his little sister whom, I could tell, for all his posturing he loved very much. So I ended up out on the floor with my leash in Angela's hand. As she knelt patting me, I wagged my tail and licked her knee and her hands, and I squirmed very glad when she tickled me.

In minutes Angela had my leash in one hand and Tinker Bell's in the other hand, and we were out the door. Freddy said "Angela!" in a pleading voice like he knew she was going to do it anyway.

It felt so good to be out of that small cage. I pranced and jumped, loving the fresh morning air and the grass under my feet. And I truly liked Angela an awful lot. She was so sweet—and determined. She walked us around the perimeter of the scraggy lawn, then led us through to the front.

Mattie was sitting on the house steps. "Poppa's not going to let you keep him, you know," he said negatively.

Angela took us to a bench by the edge of the lawn where she encouraged Tinker Bell to play with me. Mattie followed us over and sat by Angela.

"Do you want to hold him?" she asked her brother.

Mattie said, "No," like "Don't ask me again. I don't like dogs."

"You don't have to be afraid of this one," Angela reassured him.

"He's a pipsqueak," Mattie said disagreeably. My shoulder hair bristled because that's what Mack called me.

Freddy came out of the shed, looked over at us, and called out, "You're going to get me in trouble." Angela pretended she didn't hear him, and he went into the house.

25. FAMILY DIFFERENCES

A voice behind the hedge startled me. I jumped up and barked. Already I was protecting Angela.

"That's a new dog you have there, kids?" the woman asked, as she began trimming her side of the shrubbery with hedge clippers she was holding.

"Yes, Mrs. Benson," Angela answered respectfully. "He's going to play with Tinker Bell." Old Tinker Bell hadn't shown herself to be in much of a playing mood so far.

Mrs. Benson looked down over the hedge at me. "He's a cutie. What's his name?"

"His name is Topsy," Angela answered, "and he's very smart."

"He'd better be," Mrs. Benson said with a sigh, "smart enough to stay away from those monsters your dad keeps locked up. One bite, that's all it'll take for a little fella' like that. One bite and he's lunch. You better watch out for your little dogs."

"Chihuahuas don't fight," Angela explained, "only pit bulls fight."

"Yes, and it's a shame," Mrs. Benson told her. "A shame to treat dogs like that, making them fight."

"They fight because they're mean," Angela continued to explain.

"And they're mean because your dad makes them

mean. I don't know how he does it, but he's the one who makes them that way. Everyone knows what's going on; everyone, when Freddy takes them out and they see the dogs' faces. And it's against the law, you know. Your dad can go to jail for making dogs fight."

"Jail?" Angela asked, alarmed, "for letting dogs fight?"

"Well, I've said too much," Mrs. Benson replied as she moved down the hedge. "You better keep an eye on your little dogs, Angela, so they don't get bitten."

"We can't put Topsy back in the shed, Mattie," Angela said to her brother.

"Fat chance," he answered her. "Poppa won't let you have that dog."

Angela left him sitting there and led Tinker Bell and me into the house, where she went to her mother in the kitchen. "What're you doing with that dog?" was the first thing the woman said.

Ignoring the question, Angela asked her, "Why are Poppa's dogs mean, Mamma? Is it because they're big? Or does Poppa do it?"

"Do what?"

"Make them mean?"

Mamma hesitated. She thought for a moment. Then she said, "Dogs are like people, Angela. They can go either way. Some people and some dogs are not nice; some are sweet, like Tinker Bell."

"Why?"

"Well, it depends who their mothers and fathers are. Poppa wants mean dogs, so he chooses the meanest mothers and fathers for them."

"If you and Poppa were mean, would Freddy and Mattie and me be mean?"

Mamma didn't answer that question, but instead tried to reassure Angela. "So Poppa doesn't make them mean. He just brings it out of them. It's already there. Look at the wild wolves. They have to be very mean, to kill other animals; but they do it because they love their puppies and have to feed them. Like Poppa and me love you."

"So mean dogs can be nice, too, Mamma, like Tinker Bell loves me?"

"I suppose they can."

I heard the sound of Victor's car entering the driveway. He came into the house, and immediately said to Mamma, "Sophie, what's that dog doing here?" He scolded Angela for taking me out, and he said he was going to have a talk with Freddy when he got home from school. He kept calling her "Angel," and she was not afraid of him at all.

"Angel, I gave you Tinker. One dog is enough. You don't need this one."

"You have lots of dogs. Why can't I have another one?" Angela reasoned back.

"Angel, 'cause one is enough for a little girl."

"Oh, what does it matter if she plays with the dog?" Sophie objected. Then she and Victor got into an argument. Mattie walked in and began to tremble. Nobody except me noticed him.

"It matters because it's my money that bought that

dog! I don't want her getting attached to it. You want us to get laughed at? One Chihuahua running around here is enough!"

"But a shed full of pit bulls is never enough!" Sophie countered.

"I have my needs," Victor said to her dismissively.

As he scooped me up, Sophie said to him, "And your needs are going to get you in jail. And then where'll we be? Get a life!"

26. DOG BAIT

Victor took me to the shed, threw me into my cage, turned around and left. I spent a long and miserable day there. The Sheltie underneath me was still whimpering, but less and less, and slowly drifted away. Finally, she just lay there and didn't breathe anymore, like Molly's grey pup by the side of the path. When Freddy came in to feed us, he dropped her into the trash barrel.

The next morning Victor brought in a small white poodle that he put in the Sheltie's cage. She was terrified like I'd been. I made sounds to calm her.

All the dogs in the shed dozed on and off until early afternoon when Victor returned. He was greeted by his pit bulls, except Thunder who just lay watching him. Victor put Manda's four pups on leash and went out with them. Afterwards he came back and took the white poodle and me from our cages and carried us outside. Next to the house were steps that went down to a door. He took us through it into the basement.

It was a spacious single room with only a few small windows near the ceiling. All of them were shut tight, so it smelled moldy and stuffy. Manda's four almost full-grown pups were tied along a wall. A number of old chairs, some folding, some straight-backed and others stuffed and ragged, were scattered around a large circular pen.

Victor dropped the poodle into it, then tied me to the wall away from Manda's pups. He unleashed two of them and led them into the enclosure where the poodle was pressing against one side, trembling violently. The young dogs in a playful-puppy mood were curious about the little dog and went over to sniff her. One batted her with a paw. The poodle screamed as she was rolled. The other pup ran over and picked her up in his jaws and flung her like I used to do with my squeaky toys. It was a puppy game. The poodle limped up and tried to run away, but had nowhere to escape. The pups began to toss her around like a ball. They threw her in the air, grabbed her, and pounced on her. One seized the little dog by the head; the other latched onto her haunches, and they had a tug-of-war as the poodle screamed. Then they tired of their crying plaything, and went sniffing around the pen.

Victor removed the two pups, while the poodle lay off to one side, stretched where she'd landed, her body jerking. Victor led the two other pups into the pen. They ran over to the poodle, nudged her, then began to throw her around, too. One clamped on her, and the other tried to get her away from him. They ripped and tore at the little dog, so her misery was soon over. Victor let them play with the body for a few minutes. Then he took them out, and dumped it into a trash bag in the corner.

He'd saved me for the next lesson. Fight dogs don't play; they fight, one against one. Victor lifted me into the pen. Then he brought in one of the pups. I stood near the wall. The pup looked at me. He had tasted blood, and it wasn't his first time. I should've been afraid after what I'd just seen. Yes, I was tense, but not scared. The situation was somehow familiar.

I've never tried to understand my attitude, or the force I can project. I am alpha. Wherever I'd go, that place was mine—my house, my street, my city. Ted noticed my spunk in the pet shop window when I snapped at the Jack Russell that was annoying me. On the street with Ted I'd growl and jump at big dogs. He assumed I'd figured out that they were on leash like I was, so couldn't reach me. Sure, I'm "defensive-aggressive," because I'm a little guy. In my case it works.

I guess what made it most familiar facing that big pup of Manda's was my experience with Molly's pups. When they were growing up, reaching many times my size, they'd try to rough-house with me in front of the den like they did with each other. I'd have none of it, and I found that a good nip on the tip of the nose would send them running back to Molly. So this seemed more of the same.

The pup sensed that we were about more serious business because he was alone. He stood looking at me. Victor yelled, "Fight! Fight!" Then the pup walked towards me. He didn't move fast, but when he got close I did. I'm a "deer-head" Chihuahua, and as such I have longer legs, particularly my back ones, strong from running with Ted every morning and from street-living for a year. I jumped out of the way so quickly that the pup was confused. Then he advanced on me again, his head down like he was stalking me. This time as I darted away I gave him a deep bite on the tip of the nose. I didn't clamp or hold on; I was past him in a second. But the alpha in me was rousing, and I was ready to stand my ground. Anyway, there was nowhere to go. Victor was yelling, and the pup approached me again, more reluctantly, more carefully. I stood there, tensed, my haunches against the pen, and when he was one Chihuahua-body-length from me I leaped toward him and landed another good bite on the tip of his nose exactly where I'd bitten him before. I didn't jump away this time. I remained in front of him, ready to spring again, letting him know it was my pen. The pup backed off to the other side. He lay down and began rubbing his nose with his paw. I held my ground waiting.

Victor was not happy. He dragged the pup out of the pen calling him a good-for-nothing, and saying things like, "Do or die." He tied him to the wall, took another pup, the biggest one, and put him in the pen. "Ok, Tough-Nut, let's see if you can do it again," he said to me sarcastically. And I did. He watched me do it again, and by then he was yelling and yelling at the pup and at me.

Hearing the racket, Sophie came down the cellar stairs that led from the kitchen. Victor said to her furiously, "That dog is ruining my pups! That rat is ruining my pups!" He couldn't believe what had happened. "They're afraid of it! I don't know if I'll be able to train them after this." Well, that's what he got for taking on a street dog. "I'm going to feed the little crap to Thunder!"

"Could it be the pups are too young?" Sophie suggested.

"No, they're not too young! I hope they're not ruined, those two. That rat-dog!"

"Well, if you'd let Angela have him, you wouldn't be in this situation, would you? Nobody can tell you anything. Your dog bait is working better on you than on the pups; he's certainly worked you up." And she laughed at her husband and went back up the stairs. That made him really mad.

Snarling, he led the four pups out of the cellar, leaving me in the ring. When he returned for me, Sophie had come back down the stairs. "He's no use to you. Why don't you let Angela have him?" she suggested kindly. "She talks about him all the time. She really thinks he's her dog."

"No," Victor said as finally as he could. "I've got plans for this one."

"You know, you're really crazy with these dogs," Sophie said to him. "You're going to keep it up. And someday you're going to regret it."

"That's my business," he said to her as he carried me out the door.

He crossed the yard with me to the shed and, inside, flung me into my cage with such force that I lay dazed from hitting the far side.

27. THUNDER

Days dragged on, always the same routine, with nothing happening, just Freddy's feedings. The pit bulls got walked, but we stacked little dogs did not. The captives in the cages around me changed. The poodle was replaced by a toy fox terrier, that was replaced by another little poodle, a black one, that was replaced by a tan Scottie. The pit bull pups were emptying five of the six stacked cages regularly as their lessons progressed. Victor didn't put me in the ring with them again.

Day after boring day passed, but I had a consolation. One afternoon, not long after Victor had tried me out in the basement, the shed door opened. It was Angela. She came inside and tied Tinker Bell by the door which she'd carefully closed. Then she came over to my cage. "Hello, Topsy," she said. "Mamma keeps telling Poppa that he should give you to me because you're no use to him. She thinks he will after a while. Won't that be nice?" Angela petted me through the wires of my cage, and I licked her fingers. She stayed for quite a while, then said good-bye, and I went back to being bored.

The following day Angela visited me again. This time she seemed more at ease coming into the shed alone, and she said hello to all the other dogs, including Thunder. The third day while she visited me she named all the little dogs in the stacked cages. She came daily after that, and I could look forward to seeing her, until the time she noticed that Thunder had pushed his water dish out. He was lying by his wall watching her with one eye open. She moved the dish back in for him to make sure he could reach it. I barked to warn her. As she straightened up, Thunder lunged from where he lay. Only the length of his chain stopped him. He almost reached Angela. A tooth made a small rip on her blouse. That is how close he came as he jumped for her throat. Angela screamed and fell backward, safely away from him. She burst into tears, and she ran out of the shed. A little while later she came back to get Tinker Bell she'd forgotten, but she didn't stay.

I was afraid I wouldn't see Angela again. Her afternoon visits had given me something to look forward to, and I would miss them dearly. Now I could expect only long days and long nights, growing more and more cramped in my cage. Angela didn't come the next day, or the one after that. But on the third day after, I heard the shed door open, and there she was. She came in, and tied Tinker Bell by the door. She said hello to each of the pit bulls, and came over to me. She greeted each of the stacked dogs by the names she'd given them. She tickled my stomach through the wires, and I licked her fingers. We did that until reaching up got her arm tired. She talked to me and told me again I was going to be her dog and that we'd go out and play. Then she looked over at Thunder. She went and sat down cross-legged on the floor a safe distance from him. Thunder lay where he was, one eye open watching her. I felt very alarmed for my friend.

"Hello, Thunder," Angela said. "How are you today? I wish I could take you and Topsy for a walk, but you know I can't. I wish we all could be friends, you and Topsy, with me and Tinker Bell. So when I come here to see Topsy I'm going to visit you, too. Mamma says Poppa brings out your meanness; but she told me mean dogs have love, too. And I'm going to bring out your love. You can be mean with Poppa, and nice with me."

That's what Angela did the days that followed. She'd spend most of her visit with me, but then she'd sit down just far enough away from Thunder and talk to him for a while. And Thunder would watch her with one eye open. I worried every time Angela did it, afraid that any minute she'd try to pat quiet Thunder. But she didn't. She might eventually have tried if one day she thought she felt Thunder's love, I don't know. But something happened that made it impossible.

Victor was the only one who walked Thunder. Freddy fed Thunder, keeping his distance; but Victor walked him. One evening when Freddy had just put down the food dish, and Thunder was going over to it, Thunder's chain simply fell from where it had been attached to the wall. Victor hadn't secured it well that morning. Thunder and Freddy both looked surprised. Freddy stepped back slowly, but Thunder reached him in one lunge. Freddy tripped backwards, and the big dog flew over the boy, who jumped up and ran for a loft ladder affixed to the wall close by. Freddy leapt onto the ladder, and almost made it; but Thunder clamped onto his foot, and grasping his ankle like a vise, shook and pulled with all his weight to haul him down. Freddy was screaming, trying his might to hold on. Freddy screamed, and cried, and screamed.

The shed door swung open. It was Sophie. Terrified for her child, she didn't hesitate. She attacked Thunder with a shovel that stood by. Thunder turned on her and knocked her down, while Freddy scampered up the ladder. Victor came through the door and yelled a command to Thunder, and the dog went back to his section of the wall. Sophie was hysterical. "Never, never, never let my children near these dogs again!" she yelled at Victor, "or I'll see you locked up good! Don't you ever, ever forget it!"

While Victor secured Thunder, who lay down again like nothing had happened, Sophie, still very shaken, helped Freddy down the ladder. The boy was terrified, and in pain, sobbing. He had a deep gash above his shoe.

"Carry him to the house," Sophie ordered Victor. "I'm calling an ambulance," and she rushed out.

"I can drive him to the hospital," Victor called to her lamely, as he carried his son out the door, leaving it hanging open. Freddy was crying, as much from his scare as from his torn ankle.

"Then hurry up," Sophie commanded him impatiently. She rushed into the house and came right out with towels to contain Freddy's bleeding. Through the open door I saw them put Freddy into the back seat and quickly jump into the car themselves, with Sophie crying now, too, from the fright she'd had. I heard the tires screech out of the driveway.

The shed, with the door still swung open, went quiet. We all knew something major had happened. It became very, very quiet.

Sophie was true to her word. I never saw the children again, except Angela only once, the evening she saved my life. Victor came and went. He did the chores that Freddy had done. He fed us all, and he exercised his pit bulls. Like the other small dogs I'd not been out of the stacked cages in a long time; I was getting very lame.

28. FIGHT EVENT

Then one evening, when it seemed my body could stand the confinement no longer, I heard cars enter the driveway. I heard people get out of them and go towards the house, and then other mostly men's voices come up the driveway from the street. People were gathering. In a while, Victor came for Thunder. Soon later, Victor came back for me. He carried me down the outside steps into the cellar.

The room was full of men and a few women. Thunder was tied by the wall, as were two other pit bulls I'd never seen before, well-spaced from him. While Thunder lay calmly, his good side facing out, the two strangers stood ill at ease in an unfamiliar place. One was quivering, his eyes searching for someone. People were taking bottles from a shelf in a corner of the room, filling glasses, all talking and laughing at the same time. It was very loud.

Victor dropped me into the ring where I'd encountered the pups what seemed like a long time ago. I was so lame I could hardly stand. If I met the pups now, I wouldn't have a chance.

"What're you doing?" a young man questioned Victor. "Putting a Chihuahua in the pit?" like he didn't believe what he was seeing.

"An appetizer before the entrée, Berto," Victor said

with a laugh.

Another man laughed, too. "It's finger-food."

"I'm here to see a fight, a fair fight, man, not a massacre," Berto objected. "That's just cruel."

"Cruel, ha!" the finger-food jokester contested. "You're worried about cruel? Get over it, baby! How often we get to see a pit bull break a Chihuahua?" And then to Victor, "Good idea. Bring on the Chihuahuas!" And he held up his drink to the idea.

I stood in the ring, braced against the side of it. Whether it was the aching in my back or the weakness in my legs or just the hopelessness I felt, I could hardly stand. My haunches wouldn't hold me up.

"It's not a fight!" Berto protested angrily.

"You might be surprised," Victor said. And he might've been, if Victor hadn't so weakened me. I knew I couldn't run or leap; I could only wait.

Victor yelled for the people to sit down. They took seats around the pit. Some talked, some laughed, some leaned forward ready and silent, anticipating. Victor walked over to the wall and loosed Thunder. He led the big dog to the ring and put him inside it with me. The room went quiet, except for Berto who said, "You're a sick sadist, Victor. This ain't right."

"Shut up, Berto," Victor said to him.

"Yeh, shut up," other people agreed. The young man said no more.

But Thunder didn't understand what was going on. He looked at Victor to know what to do. He'd always met another dog like himself in the pit. Should he wait for the real fighter? What was this Chihuahua doing here?

"Fight!" Victor commanded him.

Thunder looked at me, then back at Victor, still trying comprehend what was expected of him. The guests began to laugh. Victor got red-faced, and very angry. He picked me up with one hand and struck Thunder in the face with me and threw me back down. He pointed at me and yelled at Thunder, "Fight!"

Maybe Thunder remembered tearing apart little dogs in the pit when he was a pup. He understood what Victor wanted him to do. He looked at me and slowly advanced. Very slowly. He was stalking me. The people gasped and spoke appreciatively to Victor and encouraged Thunder. They were about to see me destroyed in an instant, snapped like a chicken bone. Or would it be drawn out while Thunder played with me? Thunder was not the playful type. It would be quick.

The hushed room, just then, was pierced by a little girl's high-pitched shriek. It was Angela, from the top of the kitchen stairway where unobserved she'd been watching through the railing. Crying, she screamed so loud it made everybody jump up. She pleaded with her father, "No, no, not my Topsy! Not my dog! No, no, Poppa, save Topsy!" She cried and sobbed and screamed some more, "No, no, Poppa, not Topsy. Save my Topsy!" There was confusion, and all the guests looked at Victor to see what he'd do. Even Thunder became unsure, and stopped and looked around. The fact is I didn't seem to interest Thunder very much.

Victor just got more red-faced and even angrier. He

yelled back, "Sophie, Sophie, get her out of here! Why'd you let her out? Get Angel out of here!" And then to Angela, "Shut up, shut up, Angel, shut up." But Angela just kept crying and screaming.

"Sounds like you want everybody to shut up, Victor," Berto said disgusted. He reached down and lifted me out of the pit. "Here little girl, here, here's your puppy," and Berto carried me towards the stairs to Angela, who sat bent forward sobbing, her face in her hands. "Here's your puppy," Berto said to her.

Suddenly, I was lifted high in the air as Berto, totally surprised, raised his hands. Policemen came through the outside door, and two more down the kitchen stairs, guns drawn. Some people ran. Most stood with hands up. One man made it out through one of the narrow cellar windows. Victor tried to follow him and got stuck.

The commotion ended almost as fast as it began. Berto set me on the stair near Angela and raised his hands again. I didn't know what to do. Angela didn't see him bring me, because she was covering her face. Then she was almost trampled by the policemen coming down the stairs. Sophie grabbed her from above and took her away into the house. I tried to get out of the way, too. I stood there on the step while the guests were handcuffed and two of the policemen pulled Victor out of the window by the legs. I decided to go up the few steps to the kitchen.

I hid beside the kitchen counters. Sophie came by, without Angela. I followed her out the front door. The policemen were taking everyone out of the cellar. Victor appeared, handcuffed between two of them. When he saw

Sophie he asked, "Are you the one who called the cops?"

"No, the hospital called us," a policeman said, "when you brought your boy there with a dog bite. Your story was phony, why you didn't want the police notified. All we had to do is wait."

The police vans drove off with Victor and all the people. Then the white vans with orange roof lights arrived. I stood by Sophie and watched the Animal Control officers go into the cellar and come back out with the pit bulls on heavy leashes. It surprised me that Thunder was quiet when they brought him out. He followed to the van like he was out for a walk. The officers emptied the shed, too, pit bulls in one van with pit bulls, and small dogs in another van. Then they saw Tinker Bell and me with Sophie, and they took us, too. I never saw Angela again.

29. ANIMAL CONTROL

It seemed a long ride. Houses with lawns soon disappeared, and the streets became lined instead with low city buildings. We crossed the Bronx River into East Harlem. The van finally passed through a gate into a parking lot beside a wide, gray building, only a few stories high, resembling very much a concrete bunker. The officers led the pit bulls inside first, using colored rope-like leashes that looked heavy enough for the job. Then our van of small dogs was unloaded, employing on us the same surprisingly light and flexible leashes. We were brought in through the side door as the big dogs had been, but thankfully we were put into separate pens.

So Animal Control now finally had me. I felt nervous, just like when Ted used to take me to the vet. But Doctor Guarnacci always offered me a biscuit, and maybe I'd get one here, too. So I was not panicking. A cavalier spaniel, a recent arrival to Victor's cages, was terrified, though, as was the white Scottie that had occupied the cage next to mine. They weren't street dogs like me, ready for stuff happening. But then their trembling got the best of me, and I began to shake, too.

The officers who'd brought us in left us. The pit bulls settled down in their pens, resigned as they were to boring time, while we small dogs just sat and shook. Two women and a man, all dressed in white coats like Doctor

Guarnacci wore, came into the room.

"We might as well put the pit bulls down right away," the first woman said. "People don't adopt dogs with scarred faces."

The second woman, a softer person who I could sense cared more, objected, "The football player's dogs were rehabilitated. Some even became service dogs."

"They couldn't have looked as bad as these guys," the first woman answered writing on her clipboard. "Those dogs were in the news because he was a celebrity, so people wouldn't want to hear they were put down. These guys will waste our time and resources, because they'll wind up going down anyway. We don't have enough people to adopt even our qualified dogs." Then she said, pointing to Manda's pups, "We can examine those four, though. They could stand a chance."

"Poor thing!" the second woman said sadly as she looked across at Thunder's wrecked face, the bad side. "Imagine making a dog suffer that? Heartless people."

We small dogs and the four big pups were transferred to individual cages in another room where we waited, until we were taken one by one to be checked, and they saved me for last. I didn't see Thunder, or Princess or Buck or Manda again. Some time later two men in white coats walked past. One said to the other, "I've never seen a dog struggle so hard for life after injection. His heart just wouldn't stop. He fought to stay alive." Thunder?

All the small dogs were returned to their cages, one by one, except a Maltese that had been quite mangled. That one didn't come back.

When it was my turn, I was taken to an examination room like Doctor Guarnacci's, so I didn't like it, but it didn't frighten me, either. First, I was poked everywhere the same as he did. Then I was placed on the floor, and a friendly, wimpy dog brought in. We touched noses, but I wasn't feeling social, so I turned away. Then I was given some food, which was taken from me while I was still sniffing it. I didn't care. What did the woman expect me to do? Bite her hand? The other attendant tried to get me to play with a toy. Really, who'd want to play during this? He lifted me back up onto the table saying, "Seems uninterested in everything."

The woman concluded, "Bad shape physically and mentally. Hard telling how permanent the lameness is. He's a broken little dog."

"Yes, but borderline. We should ask," the man concluded.

They spoke to someone on the phone. Within minutes a stern woman walked in, also wearing a white coat. She looked at the report the two examiners had been writing. "Where's the scan?" she asked them.

"Wasn't it done?" the man replied.

"Well, it wasn't done if it's not here!" the stern woman scolded. "That's the first thing you should do!"

The man left the room quickly and came back with a device in his hand. He held it close to me and moved it over my back between my shoulders.

"There's your answer," the supervisor said. "He has a microchip. So phone the agency on the chip to contact his owner." On the way out she said, "Next time check that first!" Nobody said anything.

I was brought down a hallway to a different cage, really an individual walled-compartment with a wire gate. There were others like it all along from floor to ceiling. Some were big for big dogs; mine was small. Each held one dog. I had a bed, a water dish, a food dish, and even a toy. I waited some more, the rest of that day and through the night. It was a hallway of sighs, of sad, bored dogs. But it was a lot better than being in Victor's cage. I slept fine. I was comfortable. The short walks I was given made my legs feel better. Maybe Animal Control wasn't so bad, after all. If you have a microchip, whatever that is.

30. REUNION

The next morning, not long after I was fed and walked, and I was dozing on my bed, I heard someone stop in front of my gate. When I looked up, the light behind the person blinded me a bit, but it looked like ... Then I jumped up squealing, and wagging my tail so hard I fell over. Ted was standing there. "Hi, Sweetheart, how are you?" he said with all the love I remembered. I didn't even feel my lameness; I jumped and jumped on the gate. The attendant opened it, and I leapt into Ted's arms. I licked and licked him. "My poor Tobi, what happened to you?" he asked me. He stood up with me snuggling into his arms, and still licking him and squealing. He said to me, "My Tobi, I thought I'd never see you again, and here you are."

I jumped into my carrier Ted had brought. As we left he looked away from the rows of pens with dogs waiting for adoption. "I'd better go," he told the attendant, "their sorrowful eyes will haunt me." He signed me out, and we were on our way.

Ted carried me the several blocks to the subway where we had a long ride to Doctor Guarnacci's office. The doctor put the little muzzle on me like he always did, kissed me like he usually did, and checked me over with lots of poking while Ted held me on the table. Doctor Guarnacci concluded that all I needed was gradual exercise; otherwise I was fine. He said the luster in my coat would come back with proper diet, and lots of love. He knew I'd get that from Ted. The doctor said he was glad to know that the microchip he'd put under my shoulder skin when I was a puppy had gotten me home.

Yes, home, and that is where Ted and I headed next. Because of my lameness Ted didn't walk me across the New York University campus back to the West Village as he normally would have done. Instead, we took a cab, and I felt like a little prince again.

Ted carried me up the stairs and set me down on the landing in front of our apartment. He unlocked the door, and walked through it ahead of me. He turned back when I hesitated. "Well, you coming in?" he asked me. It was one of my little rituals; I usually waited that way for him to say something, and this time I savored the moment. Then I scurried in, into the familiar, cozy, secure feeling that had become a far memory. Here I was, finally home, after all the times I'd tried to get back here! Home!

Ted knelt inside the door to remove my harness, as always. Then he patted me and said "Good boy," as always, afterwards. And I leapt into his arms again. "Oh, Tobi, oh, Tobi, I missed you so much!" he said, holding me tight. "I missed you so much," he repeated again and again. Then he put me down.

I ran from room to room to find everything like I'd left it, my bed and little "cat house" set into the base of the bedroom bookcase, my doughnut-beds, the blue-gray one in the living room matching the blue in the carpet, and the turquoise one with all my toys around it in Ted's studio, and in the kitchen, my water dish by the stove. Everything was exactly the way I'd left it, as if we'd just returned from our walk and it hadn't been interrupted by an accident that left me on the street for almost two years. It was as if time in our apartment had stood still. That's how Ted had it ready for me. Everything was as I'd left it.

But my adventure *had* happened. Although I didn't realize it right then, home which had been my whole life before my ordeal would never be my whole life again. I'd tasted life without the leash; I'd survived, by my wits, against whatever came at me around the next corner.

With good food, and lots of sleep, with short walks, and then longer ones, I got my strength back. It wouldn't be long before I could start running again.

31. ABINGTON SQUARE

We began walking where we used to run, along Hudson River Park the length of Greenwich Village. When we passed through the northern end, I remembered Agnes. I looked around to see if I could see her, but she never was there anymore.

One afternoon outside with Ted I did find her, though. Ted likes to go through tiny Abington Square Park and sometimes sit there for a while with me on his lap. He calls it "a jewel of a park" and says it evokes memories. It is always filled with flowers. Across the street was a nursing home, and he sometimes walked me past its entrance, where benches lined the building, and residents would sit outside on a sunny day. One day on one of those benches, there was Agnes.

I stopped in my tracks so quickly that my leash pulled right out of Ted's hand. I stood there in front of Agnes, wagging my tail. She looked down at me and said, "Oh, is that you, Precious? Hello, Precious."

When Ted saw Agnes' interest in me, he let me hesitate there in front of her. He said to her, "It looks like he likes you," without ever realizing that Agnes and I already knew each other. She reached down and stroked my head. Ted said, "Oh, that's unusual. He usually doesn't let strangers touch him."

Agnes just cooed, "Precious, Precious. How are you,

Precious?"

Then we walked on. However, after that day we passed by there more often, and we stopped for Agnes every time she was sitting outside.

Mornings, when I got strong enough, Ted and I picked up our old routine. He'd walk me down Bank Street as far as Abington Square, plenty of time to do my business; then we'd continue at a run to the river. We'd jog south, following the circuit of the piers down Hudson River Park all the way to Pier 40 off Canal Street, then back up, then run across the Village on Charles Street all the way home.

One of those mornings when we were just setting out, we came upon Mack breaking into an old green Volkswagen on Charles Street near Seventh Avenue. He didn't notice us at first because we were approaching from behind him. I froze. I didn't want to go at all closer. "What's the matter?" Ted asked me, pulling on the leash. Then he realized Mack was robbing the car, and stopped, too. Probably in the mirror Mack spotted us then. He leapt out, leaving the car door hanging open, and ran away from us towards Seventh Avenue, right into the path of a police car coming down the street. The police stopped, and they must've been looking for him, because they jumped out and grabbed him. They drove off with him handcuffed in the back seat.

When we returned home, Ted phoned the police to say that he had witnessed the man breaking into a car. Then he went to the police station with me in tow to make the identification. I was quite scared at first standing in front of Mack, even though he was some distance away. He snarled at me and called me "Pipsqueak" as usual. I realized though that now I was safe because he was the one in a cage. I've never seen Mack again since then, and I hope I never will. The thought of him makes me tremble.

Days followed days once I got back with Ted, all as it used to be. With Ted I always know what to expect. Except for my memories, it was as if I'd never left. But I did have my memories when I lay on the soft fleece in my "cat house," just before dozing off. I'd found Agnes was alright and could visit her. I'd seen Mack in a cage and hope he's still there. Sometimes I thought about Molly, and how she cared for her pups. They were all five of them good dogs; she'd raised them with love. I missed them. When you've gotten used to some excitement, life can get too easy. I remembered Poor Boy and Mother. I'd been happy with them, and Sunshine. That would've been a good life, too, if it'd lasted for me. Of course, I was happiest now with Ted, but I had my memories.

32. BACK TO THE POOL

One of Ted's favorite things on a Sunday afternoon has always been a long walk in Central Park. Both of us feel very happy there. He says he finds it "so beautiful, always," and I find it so interesting, always. For Ted, "It has everything to make one's spirit soar." He'd say, "It brings me back to the countryside where I grew up, right in the middle of the greatest, most exciting cosmopolitan city in the world." He'd list what he loved about it, "Natural settings that refresh my soul, the majesty of the city towers rising beyond the trees, people talking every imaginable language on the paths, everybody happy to be out enjoying a beautiful day." Yes, Ted and I loved Central Park before I ever went there with Molly. Probably because it was closer for us, though, we always walked through the southern half, where there are the most people. It was only after I got back home to Ted, and after I regained my strength, he began to extend our walks farther up the park's west side. One lovely summer day we followed that northern path over a knoll, and Ted stopped suddenly. He stood amazed by the beauty of The Pool, my Pool, the little pond in its valley in front of us. He'd never seen it before. I was quite happy to be back there.

Ted and I continued down along the path that descends to the southern bank. We paused where a stream gushes out of the hill, flows under the pathway beneath our feet, and cascades between the rocks to the pond below. Ted took a picture of songbirds bathing along the inlet it creates. Then we walked on, the path taking us ever closer to the shoreline. Ducks and geese were swimming on the water, and flying up and having a good time chasing each other. Ted began to look for an empty bench where we could stop for a while to enjoy the beauty of the place.

Suddenly, I saw what I saw! I saw sitting on one of those benches by the path Poor Boy and Mother, with Sunshine! I was so happy, so excited! I squealed with delight and pulled on the leash to hurry Ted forward. I'm not a leash-puller, so Ted was surprised. "All in moderation," was how he liked to walk.

Sunshine saw me, too. But Sunshine was a trained guide dog now, and guide dogs don't jump up to meet other dogs. Poor Boy hadn't noticed us yet. I pulled Ted and headed for Sunshine. And there we were. I didn't know who to greet first, so I greeted them all. I went to Poor Boy, looked up at him wagging my tail, smiling my best Chihuahua smile. He was very surprised to see me. "Hobo, it's Little Hobo, Mother," he said.

"Where?" Mother asked.

"Right here in front of us," Poor Boy told her. He reached down and patted my head, then looked up at Ted questioningly.

"He obviously knows you," Ted said, surprised, his voice questioning, too. By then I'd rushed back to Sunshine and was licking his face, while he kept to his job, lying by the bench at Mother's feet, his harness easy for her to grasp. And then I jumped to Mother, placing my front paws on her knees.

Mother reached forward and patted me. "Is it really Hobo?" she asked Poor Boy.

Ted said, "His name is Tobi, Tobi Little Deer. My name is Ted. I've had Tobi since I got him as a puppy, but he was lost for two years. Maybe he met you?"

"Yes, it's Little Hobo alright," Poor Boy said, answering his mother first. Then he looked up from me to Ted again, and said to him, "He was my little dog for a while. He brought us Sunshine," and he nodded towards Mother's dog. "I'm glad to meet you. I'm especially glad to know that Hobo, Tobi, is safe." He looked back at me and, tickling me behind the ears, said, "I loved you, and I missed you."

Ted sat himself on the bench near Poor Boy with me between them. "Tell me the story. Tell me about Hobo. Tell me what happened. I'd very much like to know how he lived while he was gone away from me."

And that's what happened that beautiful bright afternoon on the south side of The Pool, sitting on a park bench facing the ledges of the Great Hill where I used to sun. Poor Boy told Ted about the first time he saw me on the street with the sign around my neck, and how he'd sighted me again right here at this little pond, with some rowdier dogs he thought I hung out with. Poor Boy told him how I'd introduced Sunshine. He recounted how he'd befriended us, and how he made arrangements with Doctor Farland just in time, before Animal Control picked us up. He described how quietly content the four of us had been, how Sunshine had gone away for training, and against the odds had succeeded. He told Ted with a shudder how Mack grabbed me on the street that fateful day.

"He ended up in a fight dog ring, for bait. That's what I learned from Animal Control who called me when they found his microchip," Ted told Poor Boy. "But I wonder," Ted asked him, "why Doctor Farland didn't check to see if Tobi had a microchip?"

"I don't know. Maybe he didn't want to find out. He knew I counted on Hobo being my dog. Nothing was settled then; we weren't so happy as now. Hobo brought us Sunshine." I licked Poor Boy's hand as he tickled me behind my ear.

"Sunshine changed my life," Mother said.

"He's changed both our lives," Poor Boy added. "Thanks to you, Hobo," he said, stroking the length of my back firmly the way I like it.

Ted and Poor Boy and Mother talked for a while more. I climbed onto Ted's lap and fell asleep in the warm sun. Yes, I was so happy to see Poor Boy and Mother again, but I was home now with Ted. I was glad to feel that, with all of them sitting there together. The memory of Poor Boy and Mother would not make me sigh any more. Now we'd all be good friends. And that's what happened. Sunday afternoons we often encounter Poor Boy and Mother and Sunshine at that beautiful pond named The Pool. We're all happy when we're together. Poor Boy and Mother call me Tobi now.

33. THOR

I think my biggest surprise of all happened one day when Ted and I were traveling by car on our way back from visiting friends upstate. Ted decided to stop at a farmer's roadside market where a big sign said "Fresh Eggs," and there were lots of vegetables, too, like our favorites, sweet potatoes, carrots, corn, broccoli and squash. When we got out of the car, right away I couldn't believe my eyes. Standing there with the farmer was Molly's Shepherd-colored pit bull pup, but not a pup anymore.

Ted held me back with my leash defensively, putting himself between me and the other dog the way he does on the street. I'd have none of that now, though, and I rushed around him and pulled to meet the dog bearing down, my tail wagging happily. Molly's pup stopped short of me, wagging his tail, too. Before Ted in his surprise could grab me up, I stretched forward and we two dogs touched noses and face-licked; I was still the dominant one. And then the pup, now a fully-grown dog but a young one, wanted to play. He invited me by jumping up and down, running a few steps and turning back to me, then stopping in play pose, back legs standing and chest on the ground.

Ted didn't know what to make of it. He never let bigger dogs come up to me. He said to the farmer, "My dog is behaving weirdly, almost like he knows your dog."

"Why don't you let him go, and let them play," the farmer suggested.

"Your dog's too big for him," Ted answered. He was annoyed that the farmer let his dog run up like that. Ted never liked to see dogs off-leash, because it made him nervous they could hurt me. Of course, he was right. But not this time.

I pulled on the leash, wagging my tail vigorously. The "pup" was jumping in and out of play position in front of us, waiting for me, his same exuberant self he'd always been. A happy, thoughtless dog, that's what'd gotten him into trouble at The Pool when he chased the ducks. Ted carefully let me get closer as it became evident the dog was no threat. Normally, I would've snarled and jumped at a big dog, a show I could safely do on leash and always was proud of afterwards; but here, instead, anybody could see I just wanted to approach this one. Why didn't Ted understand we knew each other?

"Let your dog off-leash," the farmer suggested again.

Ted didn't dare. "He's beautiful," he said admiringly to the farmer of his dog.

"Yes," the farmer replied. "The best I ever had. He's like a big playful over-grown pup. I got him to protect the chickens, and he mostly wanted to chase them himself. But he's smart; he learned."

"What's his name?" Ted asked.

"Thor, I got him a year ago on a Thursday," the farmer replied as he affectionately tickled Molly's pup under the chin. I could see that Thor loved him back very much. They were bonded, the farmer and Thor. "He's a feral dog, born wild," the farmer explained. "I found him down in New York at the city pound where a friend of mine had spotted him. He was feral, had never been in a house, so they didn't know what to do with him. They hadn't put him down yet because he had so much spirit. Probably would've eventually. That's what I was looking for, a dog who'd like living outside, and when it gets cold be satisfied with the barn, so the 'coons and foxes don't try to come into the perimeter. There're coyotes around, too, so I needed a big dog." He stroked Thor's head, "He's just a big softie," he said, as Thor smiled back.

34. AND NOW

So two of Molly's pups made it, Sunshine and Thor. What of Molly herself, and the little female Shepherd who was picked up with her? I don't know. Maybe they got adopted. Maybe the pup. But Molly? When I round a corner on the street with Ted, sometimes I expect to meet her again. But New York is a big city. Maybe somewhere she's taking care of Agnes.

Agnes? She's not at the nursing home anymore. After we didn't see her a few times, Ted asked about her. He was told that one day she went for a walk with a woman who used to visit her, and they never came back.

It's the middle of summer now. I sleep in my "cat house" most of the time in our city apartment. On Saturday mornings I jump up and down when Ted takes out my carrier for our trip to the Island. Then for two days I sleep on the front deck of our house there. Ted sets out two doughnut-beds for me, a white one in the sun and a chocolate-brown one in the shade by my water dish. I lie in the sun a lot of the time, but when I've had enough I move into the shade, then back into the sun. It's a dog's life.

Between dozing I sometimes think about my freedom with Molly. I remember our den and my afternoons sunning on the side of The Great Hill overlooking The Pool. That was the original dog's life, and I've been there.

BE MY FRIEND

Let's stay in touch. I'll be very happy to share my photo albums with you, and let you know what new adventures I might be having.

My email address is:
tobilittledeer@gmail.com

My personal website is:
http://tobilittledeer.com

My Facebook page is:
https://www.facebook.com/tobilittledeer

On Twitter:
https://twitter.com/tobilittledeer

On Instagram:
http://instagram.com/tobilittledeer

And on tumblr:
http://tobilittledeer.tumblr.com

www.ingramcontent.com/pod-product-compliance
Lightning Source LLC
Chambersburg PA
CBHW050341110726

47899CB00007B/2586